A Turbulent Tale of Love

by Shalu Thakur Dhillon

Invincible Publishers

First published in India in 2018

ISBN: 978-93-87328-77-8

Invincible Publishers

G-120, Sushant Lok III, Sector 57, Gurgaon-122002

Registered Address: Opposite Kasturba Ashram, Radaur, Haryana - 135133

Printed at Thomson Press (India) LTD

"Mera Mujh Mein Kichh Nahi,
Jo Kichh Hai So Tera.
Tera Tujh Ko Saump De,
Kya Lage Hai Mera."

To my father and late father-in-law

Acknowledgements

Great Waheguru, the greatest source of all the knowledge and wisdom, for His countless blessings.

A big thanks to my mother and my chacha ji who introduced me to the beautiful world of books.

Thank you Jas Di for making me understand the difference of perspective of an author and a reader.

Thanks to entire team of Invincible Publishers for their support.

A special thanks to my friend Deven Tyagi for a beautiful cover page idea.

Thanks to Sunil Mendiratta for his advice and support on various aspects.

I am grateful to the Armed Forces community for an enriching and fulfilling experience that came handy while writing about the various places and situations in the book.

To wrap it all, my biggest thanks of all goes to my husband Lt Col G S Dhillon and my sons Anhad and Arnav who trusted me with their never ending encouragement and enthusiasm through the creation of this book.

Prologue

Nihal, Neena and Prof. Nirmal were sitting at the dining table. The family was having dinner. Nihal's mother, Neena, had made all his favourite dishes.

"You know, Nihal, when you are around, I too get to eat good food. Else, I am served only boiled stuff," Prof. Nirmal looked at the food and said. "So much pampering for the son! Sometimes you should pamper your husband too, Neena."

"You are pampered all year round professor, where as my son is here for a few days only. As far as boiled food goes, that's only to keep you healthy and in good shape," Neena replied.

"Neena, my favourite shape is round, just like your puffy cheeks."

Before Neena could say anything, Nihal intervened, "Papa, this is what I miss the most in Bangalore; Ma's food and your jokes." He looked at his mother. "Food is amazing, ma. Yummy food, a loving mom and a doting father, what more can one ask from life?"

"You are lucky. For me, it's a nagging wife, boiled food and all those 'saas-bahu' serials. My day starts with cereal and ends with serial," Prof. Nirmal hyperbolized.

"You ignore him, Nihal. He hardly talks sense these days. Have one more chapatti." Neena rolled her eyes at Prof. Nirmal and placed a chapatti in Nihal's plate. "It seems as if you are not eating enough these days. Look at you, you are getting weaker and thinner."

"I have gained two kilos, Ma. I think I'll need to get back to my gym regime soon."

Neena made a face that made Nihal and Prof. Nirmal laugh.

"I wish my Ma were here too. Then I too would have got another chapatti."Nihal started laughing at Prof. Nirmal's quip at Neena.

Suddenly, someone pulled the dining table cloth and all the dishes went flying to the floor. Nihal turned to look around and found Niharika standing there, staring at them furiously. Nihal got scared at the sight of her. Before he could hold his mother's hand, she stepped forward and hugged Niharika.

"You need to come with me," Niharika insisted Neena. "I can't stay there all alone."

She held Neena's hand and dragged her over to the door. When they reached the door, Neena turned around and extended her hand toward Prof. Nirmal, ignoring Nihal completely.

Prof. Nirmal got up and rushed to hold his wife's hand. He looked at Nihal helplessly, but then looked away the very next moment and followed Niharika and Neena out. Nihal pleaded with his parents to stay back with him, but it seemed as if they were under some kind of a spell, not able to hear him at all. He supplicated to Niharika to leave them alone, but she gave him a cold look. Nihal and Niharika had always shared a bond of love and faith, thus he was shocked why Niharika was hell bent on separating him from his parents.

He shouted, screamed and beseeched to each one of them, but no one paid heed. One by one, all of them stepped out. Nihal found himself standing all alone in the middle of the room. Niharika had left with his parents. He ran towards the door, but stumbled over the broken pieces of crockery and his head hit against the floor. He felt as if everything around him was spinning. He tried to scream, but words seemed to have gotten stuck in his throat.

With all his might he got up, only to find that there was no one around. He was breathless, trembling and sweating profusely in his bed. The nightmare was over, leaving Nihal shaken and terrified once again.

He looked at the clock. It was three in the morning. He had a sip of water. He knew he wouldn't be able to sleep again, not that night at least, so he opened a book and started reading.

Chapter 1

Nihal, as the name suggests, was a happy-go-lucky guy. He was the only son of a Professor and a singer duo, coming from a good family, living in a posh Delhi locality, professionally well settled and personally very contended. At a glance, his life seemed to be just perfect. People used to envy him for whatever he had.

A height of above six feet, wheatish complexion, sharp features and a gym-toned body made him a head turner, an Indian version of the Greek God Adonis.

Nihal was not just about the looks, he was brains with brawn. He had a thing for reading and this hobby, for most times, gave him an edge over others when it came to debates or discussions. He had the art of putting across his point very humbly yet rationally, not making anyone feel offended. Singing had always been his forte, but now it was either books or gym that he enjoyed the most besides flying. All those qualities, combined with his profession of a pilot, got him a lot of attention, especially from the fairer sex. Right from his school days, he had been very popular among his friends as well as enemies, if he had any. Everything seemed to be in the right proportion in his life, and it was said that he was more blessed than others.

That was all about Nihal until he came across something so horrifying that changed his life completely. It not only took away his smile, music and his peace, but also gave him those bone chilling nightmares. For the past two years, he hadn't known what sound sleep, peace of mind and a happy family felt like. He always enjoyed his share of sleep in waiting lounges where he was always surrounded by a lot of people.

Seeing him struggle with life so, his father suggested for him to move away to some other city, so that he could forget the incident and start afresh. He shifted to Bangalore around a year and a half back, but that didn't change much in his life either, other than going back to the same house each day, dull and down-cast.

He drowned himself in work so that he didn't get time to think about any other thing. After long hectic gym sessions, he thought he would be able to sleep better, but none of that had helped him much.

Only a few people knew about this side of him, his weaknesses, his fears and his nightmares. Neil was one of them. He was Nihal's friend and his biggest support in that tough phase of his life.

Whenever Nihal felt low, that nothing would ever change in his life, Neil always comforted him. "Change is the only constant in this world and miracles do happen. I am sure this too will change for the better someday," he would say.

Neil knew that he was right, that Nihal's life would change, but when and how, only time could tell.

Chapter 2

One morning, a loud banging on the door disturbed Nihal's sleep. For a while, he thought it to be one of those nightmares where Niharika had come again to take his parents away with her. He hid his face in the pillow and shut his eyes tightly, but the thumping kept getting stronger and he heard Neil calling out his name. He removed the pillow, opened his eyes and looked around. No one was there, while Neil was trying to force the door open from outside.

He jumped out of bed and rushed to answer the door. The moment he opened it, Neil shouted, "Are you okay? You scared me. I thought something has happened to you."

Of course he was not over reacting. It was the first time in the last two years that Nihal had over-slept and had to be woken up. Nihal looked at the clock; it was almost seven in the morning.

"Shit…I have to report at work in an hour." He smiled briefly at Neil and hurried to the washroom.

Nihal and Neil were childhood friends. Neil was a year older to him, but was from the same school, the same neighbourhood in Delhi for many years, the same flying school and was now a pilot with the same airlines and even shared an apartment with him in the new city. Just like Nihal, he hailed from Delhi too, but Bangalore had been their new home for past year and a half.

Neil, as opposed to Nihal, was an introvert; very calm, balanced and mature. He had lost his father at a tender age and had to take up responsibilities very early on in life. At that time, Nihal and his family had stood by him and his mother. Neil, though he never said it, always felt that he owed Nihal a lot. He had a younger sister to whom he was not just a brother, but a father too. His loss had made him extremely protective about the people around him. Very religiously, he used to visit his mother and sister whenever he had an off from work and dragged Nihal to Delhi too, despite his constant excuses of not going home.

Nihal and Neil had always been the pillars of strength for each other and the bond had grown so strong over the years that they could understand even the unspoken things between them. Neil knew about Nihal's fears and insecurities very well, which was why even a slight change in Nihal's behaviour, as little as waking up late, got him worried.

Having seen Nihal alright, Neil calmed down and got busy with his morning chores too. They both had a quick bite before leaving for work. Even at the breakfast table, Neil noticed Nihal to be very quiet and lost in his thoughts. That was very unlike Nihal and it got him a little worried again.

Chapter 3

On the way to the airport too, Nihal didn't say a word. He was lost in his thoughts and had had just one thing on his mind since last afternoon, who she was and where could he find her. He was more anxious than ever now, as for the first time in the last two years, something had kept him so engaged that he forgot all about those harrowing memories and had slept like a baby.

The entire episode from the previous day flashed in front of Nihal's eyes once again. He had been waiting for his cab outside the bank. He was upset after having had a heated argument with the bank officials over the penalty of pending credit card bills, which had been a routine thing for him as he never remembered to pay them on time, until they swelled enough in numbers to worry him.

He had been engrossed in his thoughts, when a Royal Enfield stopped in front of him. He didn't pay heed to it till the biker removed the helmet. A tall and fair girl was standing in front of him and her long hair fell loose over her face when she pulled the helmet off. She was dressed in a smart pink formal shirt and trousers. There was something about her that glued his attention to her. She parked the bike and started walking towards the building he had just come out of.

Nihal wished for her to turn back at least once so he could see her pretty face again, but his cab arrived just then. He sat in the cab and turned to have a last look at her. She spoke to one of the security guards for a minute and then walked into the building after politely acknowledging the guard's salute. Before he could understand anything or react, the taxi moved forward.

Nihal seemed to have frozen in that moment, as he couldn't think of anything but her since then. The face was too pretty to be forgotten. That night, lying in his bed, he was thinking about her and didn't realize when sleep dawned upon him.

Like any other night, he had one of those nightmares that night as well. Niharika had come to take his parents with her. Nihal screamed and begged his parents to stay with him. He ran and held his father's hand and tried to stop him.

However, something unusual happened in his dream that night. A girl in a pink dress came from somewhere and held Nihal's hand. That gave Nihal courage and he held his father's hand even more tightly. His mother looked at her husband and instead of going with Niharika, she chose to stay back with her husband too. Niharika simply stood and looked at all this. She waited for some time, insisting Nihal's parents to come with her, but when they didn't concede, she left angrily.

After Niharika left, the girl in the pink dress held Nihal in her arms and put him to sleep, only to be woken up the next morning. She was the same girl whom Nihal had seen outside the bank the previous afternoon.

The day passed by like any other day. Nihal had to fly to many cities. On the way while flying low, he saw thousands of people below, but the question bothering him all this time was where could she be? By the time he landed back in Bangalore, he knew what he was supposed to do. From the airport, he took a cab back to the same place, went inside the bank and scanned the entire place, but she was not there. He thought of enquiring about her, but didn't know what to ask and from whom. Who was she? What was her name? Miss Pink Shirt? He was not even sure if she worked there, or had simply been a visitor like him.

Disappointed, he stepped out of the building and was about to leave when someone caught his attention - the guard whom she was talking to the day before. He rushed to him and asked him about the girl he had seen the day before, the one who had come on a bike, was tall and beautiful and was wearing a pink shirt and trousers. The guard gave him a puzzled look and turned down his enquiry, saying that he knew nothing. That killed his last hope to reach her. Nihal tried to remind him, but the guard kept rattling the same answer, that hundreds of people visited the place throughout the day, so he remembered nothing. At last, he called for a cab and left for the place he had been calling home for the last few months.

Back home, he found Neil already there and waiting for him. Neil quickly made a cup of coffee for Nihal and handed him the cup. Settling on the sofa next to him, he asked, "For once, will you tell me what is bothering you and why you left from airport without me?"

Nihal made a quick excuse that he had to go to the bank and started sipping his coffee, still looking lost. Neil knew that something was bothering his friend, but he didn't want to poke him too much. So he got up saying that if there was anything Nihal wanted to share, he was around, and left for the kitchen to see what was there for dinner, leaving Nihal alone with his thoughts.

After sometime, Nihal got up too and went to the kitchen to sit over the counter.

"I don't know if what I am going to tell you will make any sense, but it's certainly unusual," he started and told Neil what all had happened with him since the previous afternoon and why he got up late that morning.

Neil was quite surprised to hear it too. He then asked if Nihal had seen or remembered the licence plate of the bike.

Nihal shook his head. "It all happened so quickly that I couldn't notice anything besides her. May be that is why she was in my dream too."

"Don't worry, we will work something out, but for now, let's have dinner." Neil patted his back and tried to comfort him.

He noticed that even Nihal's favourite chicken biryani could not bring a smile to his face.

That night, Nihal set an alarm for the next morning before getting into bed. Thoughts of her flooded his mind again.

"Where are you Ms.Pink shirt and long hair? Where can I find you? Are you real or just an illusion?" He kept thinking about her and didn't realize how and when he dozed off. No nightmares bothered him that night and for many nights to follow.

Chapter 4

A few days passed by. Nihal and Neil went back to that bank's building a few times, but they couldn't get any information about Ms. Pink shirt. Even the guard didn't seem to have any clue about her. But the one thing that both Neil and Nihal noticed was that the guard always looked nervous whenever they asked him about her, and at several occasions had tried to avoid them too. His statements were conflicting as well. Nihal was sure that the guard had some clue about her, but was not willing to tell them the truth.

One day, when he had an off from work, he reached the same spot where he had last seen her. He scanned the entire parking lot for a Royal Enfield. To his disappointment, there was none and even the guard was not there. He sat down on one of the bikes parked there while thinking of what to do next, when he saw the same guard approaching from the other side. He rushed towards him, caught him by his arm and dragged him to a corner.

Before he could ask anything, the guard asked, "Why are you looking for that girl? What business do you have with her?"

"I have to meet her and it's urgent," Nihal replied.

"It's not good to harass people. She comes from a good family and it isn't right to enquire about her like this," the guard said and tried to look away.

For once, Nihal was not irritated but relieved as he became sure that the guard knew something about her. He kept his calm and pleaded with the guard to divulge the information he had about her, while stuffing a Rs. 500 note in his pocket.

Initially, the guard was reluctant and said, "I can't tell you anything about her. She comes from a good family and is well placed here. It can cost me my job too."

Nihal held him by his shoulders and looked into his eyes, "I too am well placed in an aviation company as pilot. I too come from a good family."

The guard gave him a puzzled look and finally said, "Her name is Rabani Singh. She used to work here in one of the offices in that building, but has now shifted to some other place. That's all I know about her."

"Hmm, just try to recall any other detail that you might remember about her," Nihal insisted.

The guard scratched his forehead as if trying to remember something. "She is from Delhi," he said.

"Anything else?"

"Sir, once I was very sick. She noticed it and gave me some money and asked me to go see a doctor. When I tried to return the money, she didn't take it. She is very kind, else who bothers so much about a poor guard. That is why I didn't tell you anything about her. Today as well, it is not about the money you gave me. It's because you have come looking for her so many times and you sound very genuine," the guard said and tried to return the money, but Nihal stuffed the note back in his pocket.

In the end, he said that he expected Nihal to be a gentleman and would do her no harm. Nihal hugged him and assured him of it.

Nihal felt a sense of achievement. He was excited about this little development. She was no longer Ms. Pink shirt. She was Rabani; her name as beautiful as she herself was, he thought. Though this was not enough to find her, Nihal was happy that he knew at least something about her. The frown lines on his forehead vanished and he was smiling again. He had his lunch, a full meal after many days, and finished some household shopping and chores which usually Neil handled, since Nihal found it too boring and always conveniently passed on to him.

When Neil came back in the evening, he was surprised to see a different Nihal, a smiling and cheerful version of him. Over a cup of coffee, Nihal told him all about the new development on Ms. Pink shirt. He was happy on finally getting to know something about her. In his excitement, he failed to notice the sudden silence that had fallen upon his friend. After a while, Neil excused himself and retired to his room.

That night, Nihal found him thinking about her again. It had become a routine, but today he had a reason. She was no longer Ms. Pink shirt, she was Rabani.

"Rabani," he whispered. "What a beautiful name for a beautiful girl! A divine message from god," he smiled. "Is it because of her that I have my peace of mind back? I no longer have those nightmares. It seems now that I have a reason to live, something to look forward to," he kept thinking. "Is this a sign from Him? If He wishes it, I will surely find her some day." Nihal assured himself.

However, there was one strange thing which Nihal didn't realise. Neil never brought up the talk of Rabani again.

Chapter 5

Time was flying and Nihal was nowhere close to finding Rabani, but the thought about her every night without fail. "Where the hell are you, Rabani? When will I get to see you again?"

One of those days, he had to travel to Hyderabad to attend a friend's wedding.Since his flying hours for the month were already done, he had three days off and was to report back to work on Tuesday. As it was a long weekend, he thought of visiting his parents in Delhi too, since it had almost been two months since he last visited them.

All those days, he didn't want to go back to his house. He was scared that the nightmares might come back. But how long could he have kept avoiding it? They were his parents and he was the only one for them, he thought. Going home felt more like a punishment to him– an ailing and broken mother, a quiet father and the sombre memories of old days. All that made Nihal feel depressed and low. Since the guilt of being indifferent towards his own parents was weighing him down, he decided to go home.

It was an evening flight from Hyderabad to Delhi. August rains had made the weather pleasant in Hyderabad. Nihal entered the airport and started walking towards his airline's office to check for the availability of a seat. Something caught his attention there. For a while, he thought he was hallucinating. This couldn't be her! He had only seen her for a minute that day, and then in his dreams for almost every night since then, and now at the airport after almost a month and a half. The same pink shirt and black trousers, long hair braided neatly - surely it was her, getting her baggage scanned at a counter. Nihal tried to read, she was at his own airline's counter. 'But where is she going? Delhi? No? Yes?'

He rushed to his airline's office and checked for seat. He finished the formalities quickly with an eye still on her. Out of curiosity and excitement, he asked the man on duty if he could tell him where Ms. Rabani Singh was travelling to, and hoped like hell that he would say Delhi. The man pressed a few keys and told him that she was indeed going to Delhi. "Seat number 6 F."

"Is the flight full?" Nihal's heart was beating fast.

"Not really," he replied. Nihal asked him if he could manage to keep the seats next to her vacant. He smiled and said that it would be done. Nihal thanked the guy and proceeded to the security check. He couldn't believe that it was happening for real, that he had not only found her but was also going to be with her soon.

He settled in the corner seat at the waiting lounge. She was sitting two rows away, facing him, lost in a book with not the slightest clue that she was being watched.

The boarding was announced. She was one of the last few to board, while Nihal was the last one. As he boarded, a few known faces welcomed him. He hurried towards the sixth row and to his joy, all the seats in her row were vacant. She had settled down by then and was lost in her book again. He quickly grabbed the aisle seat, as if someone else was going to take it if he didn't hurry up.

She gave him a quick look and returned to her book again. It was the same book which he had finished reading just a few days back. Very neatly, she had placed her boarding pass as the book mark.

"Nice book," he said.

She looked back at him. "Sorry?"

"Nice book," he repeated, pointing at the book.

"Yea, I am yet to finish it." Her beautiful eyes turned to him once again.

"Hi, I am Nihal."

She looked at him, nodded, but kept quiet. This was the first in a long time that his charm hadn't worked on a girl. He decided not to bother her for some time. The plane started to taxi, while Nihal's brain raced faster than the plane on how to seek her attention and break the ice.

The plane took off. They both were lost; she in her book and he in his thoughts. After a while, she got up from her seat and opened the overhead bin. She tried to pull out her bag, but it had got entangled with the other bag there, so she couldn't pull it out.

Nihal saw her struggling and got up. "May I?"

She pulled her hand out and Nihal pulled the bag out for her.

"Thanks," she said and settled down in her seat. He acknowledged it and settled down as well.

"You seem to be an avid reader," he said. "Are you a writer?"

"No, I work for an HR company," she said, not even look up. It made Nihal uneasy that this conversation was not going anywhere.

"So, what else do you like other than HR and reading?" He was trying hard to strike a conversation.

"Music," she said without looking up.

"What kind of music?" he asked.

"Sufi, country and *gazals* too," she replied hurriedly. "If you don't mind, I want to finish my book."

"Well, I can help you with that," he suggested.

"How?" she looked at him.

He, in no time, narrated the entire story to her. Her expressions changed immediately and she looked at him disgusted. "You are impossible." Shaking her head, she tucked the book in the pocket in front of her seat, and closed her eyes as if trying to sleep.

He looked at her for a while and then said, "Hey, listen. I was only trying to save your time, so we could talk once you were free from your book."

She kept quiet.

"Okay! Shall we try some music then?" Nihal wanted the conversation to go on, but she neither replied nor did she open her eyes. He waited for a minute and then started humming an old song from a famous movie, *Ek Ajnabi Haseena Se Yoon Mulakaat Ho Gayi.*

She heard him singing, but didn't react. Rather, she pretended to be sleeping. He finished the song and knew very well that she was listening to him.

"A music lover, yet no appreciation!" he mumbled and waited for her to react, but she didn't say a word and kept her eyes shut.

Soon, she was fast asleep. Now, Nihal had all the time and liberty to have a good look at her. "Beautiful would be such an understatement," he thought, "But why are you so indifferent towards me? I have been waiting to see you for weeks and here you are sleeping, not even bothered to look at me. That's not fair. It's not your fault though, you don't know me, but I bet that once you get to know me, you won't be able to resist me."

He quietly took out her book from the pocket and scribbled a few words down on the last page. "Sorry, I didn't want to ruin the joy you were having reading this book, but I couldn't resist talking to you. Anyway, it was nice meeting you, Nihal." He wrote down his phone number too. He kept the book back, took out his phone and quietly clicked a picture of the sleeping beauty. "Now you will be in front of my eyes all the time, not just in my thoughts."

The pilot announced the landing soon after and she woke up. He smiled at her, but she still seemed to be mad at him.

"Look, I am sorry. I didn't mean to offend you. I had nothing to do, so I thought perhaps we could make some conversation," he paused to see her reaction. "Usually, I am a very well behaved man, but I don't know what got into me today. I know it was not good on my part and I sincerely apologize for it," he said with a childlike innocence.

She started smiling. "That's alright." The guy was too handsome and too polite to be mad at for long, she thought.

"I guess I was bad company," he said, but she shook her head in response.

The plane landed. He got up and took out the things from the overhead storage and handed them over to her. They alighted the plane and started walking down towards the luggage belt together. Nihal didn't realize it, but he was spell-bound walking with her. Rabani noticed it too and found it awkward, but to her surprise, she didn't dislike it.

"How are you planning to go home? It's late and Delhi is not very safe for a girl travelling alone at such late hours."

She informed him that she had someone coming to pick her up. Nihal was disappointed. He waited while she collected her luggage, and the time finally came to say goodbye. She was about to say something, but her phone buzzed just then and she got busy with the call. He heard her asking the person on the call to get the car to the exit.

Unwillingly, he had to let her go. His only hope now was the message he had left in her book. He was not sure, however, if she would read it and respond. Nihal saw her going away. He called for a cab and started for home.

Chapter 6

Nihal reached home, that same old sad looking place. The house, which at one time had been full of life, now looked quiet and murky. He wondered how anyone could live there anymore. He rang the doorbell. His father opened the door and hugged him instantly. A sudden sense of sorrow and guilt dawned upon him that he couldn't do anything for his parents.

His father enquired about his well being and Nihal took a quick update from him on his mother's health. She was sleeping after having had her medicine. He had dinner with his father and joked that his cooking had really improved. His father smiled and tried to make him feel welcome.

Nihal's father, Prof Nirmaljit Singh Bajwa, a physics professor, was a renowned name in his field. He had been a professor at Delhi University, but had resigned from his job two years ago to be with his ailing wife and to share her grief and pain. Through those years, he tried his best to soothe her and make her happy. He learnt to do all the household chores himself and completely forgot his own pain and suffering for the sake of his wife and son. In fact, he was the one who had suggested Nihal to shift to some other city, seeing him struggle with the situation at home, so that he could manage to move on with his life.

After dinner, they kept talking for some time. He could see that his father was delighted to see him.

"You should go and relax now," said Prof. Nirmal after a bit of chit chat.

He came to his room. All his things were neatly kept, the way they had always been. He freshened up, changed and slipped into his bed. He kept thinking about his father and how he was struggling with life. This made him sad.

His thoughts then wandered over to Rabani again. He still couldn't believe that he had actually met her and was with her for a few hours. They had hardly spoken, but her presence really comforted him; her eyes, her gestures, even her indifference towards him, and the song he hummed. He jolted up from his bed when he realised that he had sung after two whole years. She was doing these strange things to him and he was just following her by instinct. In the previous two years, he had not touched his guitar or sang anything, as it brought many unpleasant memories with it.

'But this girl! Oh God! What is she doing to me?' He longed to see her again, but how?

He checked his phone's contact list to find the number of the guy he had met a few days back, the one who worked at the software department of his airlines. He tried to recollect his name—Ajay. Nihal knew that if she had come to Delhi on a weekend, she would surely go back too, but where? Hyderabad? Bangalore? This guy could surely help him find out, he thought, and dialed his number. He then looked at the clock and realised that it was really late, so he disconnected the call.

Within a few minutes, Ajay called him back. He had perhaps been awake. Nihal explained the situation to him and asked if he could help him find out about this girl, Rabani Singh, who would be flying from Delhi to either Bangalore or Hyderabad in a day or two. It was personal, he mentioned. The guy assured him that he would get back to him the next day with the information. Nihal felt relieved and was sure that he would see her again soon.

Rabani was in her bed, thinking about the stranger she had met on the flight - a tall, handsome, pleasant looking man who could stop you in your tracks, with broad shoulders, a nonchalant gaze and a soulful voice, though a bit childish at times. He could be the stuff of any girl's dreams. She had been irritated with him that time, but she regretted it now.

"I should have listened to him. He was so cute." She turned in her bed. "But why was he being so friendly? Was he just another creep too, like the ones I keep meeting every once in a while? Their aim is just to flirt," she thought for a minute. "No, he didn't look like one," she argued with herself for him. She kept thinking about him till she fell asleep.

The next morning, Ajay called Nihal up with the information that the girl was a frequent flyer with their airlines, and that she would be flying to Hyderabad by the Monday morning flight. He gave him the flight details. Nihal thanked him and asked if he also knew her seat number. He smiled as Ajay told him the number to be 6F. The very next minute, he booked himself on the same flight, seat 6E. 'It's Monday morning and the flight might be running full. I can't take a chance,' he reasoned with himself.

Nihal spent the day with his parents. He realized how happy they were with his presence, and he felt happy and contended too. His mother seemed a little relaxed that day and was interestedly taking part in their conversation. It had been quite long since they all sat down like a family to spent time together. He got remorseful when he realized that he had become so lost in his own life that he had hardly been there for his parents. He decided that he would visit them more often in future.

Chapter 7

It was Monday morning. Nihal reached the airport, but was not sure how she would react on seeing him. He finished with the check-in formalities and settled in a corner. He looked around for her, and there she was, looking gorgeous in a green shirt and black trousers. The boarding started and he was the last one to board. The cabin crew greeted him and he spent a few minutes with them before settling down.

"Good morning," he smiled at her.

She looked at him shocked. "Hello."

"So, we meet again. Going back to work?" he smiled. "I hate Monday mornings."

'God! Why am I ogling at him?' Rabani realised. She hastily put on her earphones and started adding tracks to her playlist. She too was excited to see him again, but didn't want him to know it.

He thought that she did this to avoid a conversation, but her presence alone was enough to make him happy. The plane took off, he picked up the newspaper and started going through the headlines.

She got up from her seat and asked to be given the way. She wanted to use the lavatory.

He pointed towards the seatbelt sign and said, "You can't go, the weather is bad. You will have to wait."

"But I need to go now," she whispered.

"The air-hostess won't let you, ma'am."

"That's my business, I can deal with it," Rabani rolled her eyes.

The plane shook vigorously just then and she banged her head against the side panel. She had to hold the seat in front of her to steady herself.

"See, you can't go right now," Nihal said. "So please sit down. I am sure you can deal with the airhostess and the turbulence too, but you don't need to prove it."

Annoyed, Rabani sat down. Since she had no choice, she closed her eyes.

"If you want, I can help you. You know, I am good at that," Nihal said, but she didn't reply.

"So, who all are there in your family back at home?" he asked after waiting for a minute.

"My parents, an elder brother and a sister," she replied briefly.

"You are the youngest at home?" His gaze was fixed at her.

She nodded.

"You are from Delhi, right?" he asked.

She looked up at him with her big eyes. "Yes, I am from Delhi. Both my siblings are pilots. My dad is retired from the army. My mom is a home-maker. I work for an HR firm in Hyderabad. I was home for the weekend. I had a great time at home. Now I am going back to work. I think that is enough, or is there anything else you want to know?" She sounded irritated.

Whether it was because of his incessant questions, or her need to use the lavatory, Nihal couldn't understand. He started laughing, "Yes, one more thing. Is this bad mood of yours an eternal problem, or is it some special occasion today?"

She looked at him as if wanting to say something, but ended up smiling.

"That's good," he said. "You should smile more often. Firstly, it looks good on you; secondly, it brightens up other people's day; and thirdly, it can calm the weather Gods too."

She looked away but kept smiling.

"How about coffee?" he asked out of the blue.

"Coffee?" She turned to look at him.

"Yea, coffee."

"You mean now? How is this possible?" She frowned.

"Now, later, here or somewhere else; whatever you say. I am very flexible like that." He was starting to enjoyher irritation.

"No, thank you," she replied firmly.

"Bad luck." He made a sad face.

She shot him a glance.

"Coffee's bad luck, I mean."

She couldn't stop smiling at his quick retort.

"There you go." He made way for her and pointed towards the overhead panel. "The seatbelt sign is off, you can use the lavatory now."

She looked at him and then at the overhead panel.

"Hurry up before it gets too crowded there," he said and looked around.

She got up quickly and rushed towards the lavatory.

"Thanks," she said before settling down in her seat when she came back. Nihal acknowledged it and sat down too. "See, I told you it helps."

"What?" she frowned.

"Your smile," he paused. "It can certainly calm the weather Gods down, any God for that matter."

"You know, you are impossible," she said and shook her head.

"Not really," he replied.

Once again, she stuffed her ear phones into her ears and switched on some music. She didn't want Nihal to know or feel that she was actually enjoying his attention or the conversation.

They landed in Hyderabad and switched on their phones. She checked her phone and dialed a number. He heard her talking about some meeting in Bangalore the coming Thursday. 'So, she will be coming to Bangalore on Thursday.' He was yet to start thinking of how to meet her again, but before he could move a finger, he had got a clue.

It seemed as if the entire universe was with him on this one thing at least.

"Thanks and goodbye," she said before leaving.

"We might meet again, you never know," he replied and they left for their respective destinations; she to her office and he to Bangalore. She left a little more puzzled this time, and he a little more confident.

Back home, he narrated the entire story to Neil, who was equally surprised at how things had progressed. "Wait for Thursday, best of luck," he said.

Nihal checked his schedule and saw that he was not flying on Thursday. There was a message on his mobile saying," Ms. Singh is flying from Hyderabad to Bangalore on Thursday morning." The flight details were attached along with the text. It was from Ajay.

'The guy is doing a good job,' Nihal thought to himself and texted him a thank you message.He couldn't resist planning his next journey. All he looked forward to the entire week was 'Thursday morning'.

Chapter 8

On Thursday, Nihal took the early morning flight to Hyderabad, to come back to Bangalore with Rabani. He tried to sleep, but sleep was far from his eyes that day. Besides, he was little unsure about her reaction. They were going to be co-passengers third time in a row. How she would react to this- happy, annoyed, surprised or shocked, he was not sure. At the Hyderabad airport, after finishing the security check, he picked a seat slightly far away from the boarding gate so that she would only see him in the flight.

As usual, he boarded at the end and spent some time chit-chatting with his colleagues; he knew almost the entire cabin crew. This time he was a little nervous too, what if she reacted inappropriately to him being there again, that would be embarrassing. But he pushed the thought aside, thinking that he could handle that and started walking towards the 6th row.

As expected, this time she was really shocked to see him. She knew that it was not a coincidence anymore for sure. "What is this guy up to? Why is he always around me? Am I being followed or stalked?" Though Nihal didn't look like a stalker, but the thought was certainly very scary.

Nihal took out a book, his ear phones and an eye mask and tucked them neatly in the pocket in front of his seat. "I thought in case we meet again, I should be well equipped to travel with you."

She was sure that he knew she would be on board. "What the hell is this? Are you stalking me? What business do you have with me? And how the hell did you know that I am travelling to Bangalore today, that too by this flight and seat number?" She shook her head in disgust."I took you for a decent man but this is what you do?"

He was quiet as he didn't know what to say. After a minute, he raised his hand to press the buzzer over her seat. An airhostess appeared and asked her if she needed something. She remained quiet and shook her head. He smiled at the airhostess and asked her for two glasses of water. She nodded and left to get the water.

He looked at Rabani and said, "Why didn't you report it? I would have been thrown out of the plane immediately and could even be arrested for stalking a girl."

Rabani looked at him in surprise.

He looked straight into her eyes, "Do I look like a stalker? Have I ever been disrespectful or insolent? Is greeting someone you know a crime?" He paused as the airhostess returned with two glasses of water. He took both the glasses and handed over one to her. "I won't bother you for anything. If you don't want it, you will never see me again. It's only a matter of a few minutes. Once we reach Bangalore, I will be gone, never to come back again."

Her eyes welled up. This was the last thing he had expected. Everything was going wrong. He didn't consider it to go this way. “Please don’t cry. I won’t say a word now, I promise. I didn’t come to see you crying.” He got up and took a vacant seat on the other side of the aisle. He shut his eyes and rested his head back on the headrest. Meanwhile, the plane had taken off.

She looked at him. He seemed really upset. She was looking at him properly for the first time. He didn’t seem to be a creep; a pleasant face, high cheekbones, an angular jaw—any girl could fall for him easily, though his heart warming smile was missing today; impaired by her words, she thought. In fact, every time they had met, he was respectful, gentle and well behaved. 'Nihal, a name as pleasant as he himself is.'

She felt sad and repentant at the same time for her behaviour and wanted to apologize, but he was sitting far away now. In fact, for the last few days she too had been thinking about him and to some extent liked him being around. She decided that she would speak to him once they reached Bangalore.

However, as soon as the plane landed, he got up from his seat and moved towards the exit. He didn’t even look at her. The gates opened, he moved out and disappeared. She didn’t get a chance to speak to him, let alone apologise. She walked towards the exit, called for a taxi, and left for her office.

For the next two days, she thought about nothing but him, while he felt embarrassed and regretful about whatever happened that Thursday morning. Lost in her thoughts, mechanically she finished her work and caught a flight back to Hyderabad. As she settled in her seat, she noticed the seat next to her was unoccupied. 'He might come in a few minutes,' she thought. She waited till the last minute for him to be there. The doors closed and the plane started moving. He was not there with her that day and she felt terrible.

The memories of the previous day flooded her mind again. How could she have been so stroppy, she rued. The plane landed in Hyderabad. It was dark outside, she looked through the window, but it was darker inside her. She realized that she missed him.

As the people started moving, she got up from her seat and started walking slowly towards the exit. And then she saw him again. He was standing in the doorway with the cabin crew, in a pilot's crisp uniform and talking to an airhostess. 'God! He looked so handsome, more than ever!' Rabani's heart skipped a beat. She rushed to him. "Hello," she managed to say. She couldn't believe her eyes.

"Hello ma'am I hope you had a comfortable flight."

She was mortified. She tried to say something. But it was not an appropriate place and other people were waiting for her to move ahead. She nodded and walked out of the plane. He saw her going and felt sure that she was not the same girl whom he had met the day before. Something within her had changed certainly. She had missed him not being around that day and it was written all over her face.

"See you soon." He regretted being harsh on her.

Chapter 9

Back home, the first thing he did was to call up Ajay and find out about Rabani's next travel plan. He assured to get back as soon as he would get to know.

The next few days, her sad face kept bothering him. He longed to see her again. Since he didn't hear about any travel plans of her, he felt restless. In a way it was good, he thought, let he be missed.

At last, he got the much awaited message that she was coming to Bangalore again on the following Thursday and then flying to Delhi on Friday. He was free that weekend. He called his father up and told him about his weekend plans. Nihal was going home for the weekend.

For the rest of the week, he was happy and excited to meet Rabani again. He was sure to see a different side of her this time. On Thursday, Neil asked him to join him for dinner as his fiancée's sister was in town and he was taking her out for dinner, but Nihal refused as he didn't want his mood to be spoiled that weekend. "Your fiancée is never happy to see me and I am sure her sister will be no different."

Nihal had flying on Friday, but he was hopeful to be back by evening. He didn't book a seat this time and thought of trying his luck with getting a seat, or manage with a jump seat otherwise. On Friday, he was all set to go to Delhi. He boarded the flight, but sat two rows away from Rabani. He had made sure that the seats in his row were all vacant. He wanted her to approach him this time, if she so wanted, which he was sure that she would. He ignored her completely, as if he didn't know that she too was on board. She spotted him as he was settling down and felt relieved, "Finally, he is around again."

The plane took off and she waited for things to settle. She got up from her seat then and pretended to go to the lavatory. On her way back, she stopped to sit next to him. "Hello Nihal," she started the conversation.

"Hello ma'am, how are you?"

"I am sure you know that my name is Rabani."

"Yes, I do. But you see, since you never told me your name, I thought it would be inappropriate to address you by your name," he said.

She realized how rude she had been to him all this time.

"You seem to be really mad at me." She looked at him, but he was still not looking at her.

'You stupid girl, I am not mad at you, I am simply mad about you, he thought to himself and tried not to smile.

"Look, I am sorry for whatever happened that day. It was just that I was not expecting you to be there. Frankly speaking, I was a bit scared too," she conveyed her point.

"That's okay, Rabani, I understand."

"Going home?" she asked.

He nodded. The equation seemed to have changed; that day, she was leading the conversation.

"So, you too are from Delhi?" she said.

"Hmm." He was brief.

"And you are a pilot?"

"Yea," he nodded.

"Who all are there in your family at home?" She was trying hard to keep the conversation going.

"Parents," he said, still not looking at her.

"Only child?" she tried yet again.

He nodded and closed his eyes, wishing if only she was right, then things would have been so different at home. His parents wouldn't be suffering so much then. She waited for him to respond. When he didn't reply, she got up saying that she was sorry for that day, and returned to her seat.

He opened his eyes to find her gone. He looked back; she was in her seat, looking out of the window and seeming a bit disappointed too. He got up, went to her seat and sat down next to her. She seemed low. "Don't think too much, Rabani. You didn't overreact that day. In fact, you were right; I was actually stalking you. It couldn't have been a coincidence each time, but believe me, I didn't mean any harm. I like you, so I was trying to get to know you a bit more," he said confidently. "And I am not sorry for anything but one that I made you cry that day. I sincerely apologize for that."

She was surprised at what he said and the ease with which he said it. She tried to speak, but didn't know what to say.

"Will you be in Delhi for the next two days, Rabani?"

She nodded.

"If it's okay with you, can we meet tomorrow?" he asked.

"My sister is getting married in a few days, so I would be busy shopping with my family this weekend," she spoke at last.

"It's okay, Rabani. Still, if you change your mind, you have my number."

She looked up in surprise.

"It is written behind the book you were reading that day." He looked into her eyes.

"And you must be having my number too?" she asked.

"Not at the moment. Even if I had it, I would never use it without your permission, Rabani."

"But why do you want to meet me?" she was curious.

"That I will tell you when we meet next," he smiled at her.

"Why me?" she frowned.

"Because you are special," he whispered.

She was quiet after that, struggling hard to decipher what he meant.

The plane landed. "I will wait for your call, Rabani. Hope I won't have to wait for long," he sighed. "I have no other way to reach you." He got up and left for his seat to collect his luggage.

"Nihal," she called out. "That book of mine is back in Hyderabad." She unlocked her phone and handed it over to him. He saved his number in her phone and returned it to her.

"Thanks," they both said together and started laughing. He was sure that she would call sooner than he thought. At the airport, they collected their luggage and started walking towards the exit. As usual, someone was there to pick her up.

"I will wait for your call, Rabani. Don't make me wait for too long," he reminded her. She nodded and left.

Nihal was happy. It seemed as if all his prayers were finally being answered.

Chapter 10

After a long time, Nihal entered his house with a smile on his face. Since he had informed of his arrival before hand, his parents were waiting for him. His mom was awake and his father informed him that his mother had prepared dinner for them that day. Nihal hugged her and realized how much his parents missed him. He regretted his decision of shifting to Bangalore.

They sat down for dinner and his mother too joined them that day. He looked at his mother. She had been so beautiful once, but the last two years had aged her suddenly. He wished that if only he could omit that one incident from their lives, things would be so different. He didn't want to think about that again, so he brought himself back to the ongoing conversation. They kept talking for a long time even after dinner. Then his father asked him to go to his room, thinking that Nihal must have had a long hectic day.

As he got into bed, the events of that evening started playing in front of his eyes, frame by frame. He felt sure that she would call soon. "You are so close yet so far, Rabani. Call up." He shut his eyes and tried to sleep.

Rabani too reached her home, thinking about him all that time. Everyone was waiting for her at the dinner table- her mom, dad, sister and brother-in-law to be. She hugged everyone briefly, freshened up and settled in one of the chairs. The entire conversation that evening was centered around her sister's wedding preparations, as her brother-in-law to be was there too. She was trying hard to concentrate, but her mind was elsewhere. Her brother-in- law to be was a long time family friend, so they were very comfortable with him already.

After dinner, her mother got busy with winding up the kitchen and her sister went to make coffee. Her father, as usual, got busy watching the news. She and her brother-in-law were left alone. "Thanks for meeting me this time, otherwise you come to Bangalore and don't even bother to inform me, let alone visit me," he complained.

"You are busy flying most of the time and then you have someone sharing the apartment with you too, so I didn't find it too appropriate to bother you," she replied. "Can I ask you something?"

"Sure, go ahead," he said.

"But it will remain between you and me."

He nodded to assure her.

"Do you know a guy named Nihal?" she asked.

Her brother-in-law was alarmed. "Why, what happened? All well?"

"Nothing, I just met him on the flight. Since he said he works for same airlines as you, I thought I'd ask you."

"But then, why does it have to be a secret?" he frowned.

"No, it's just…you know Mannat, she over reacts most of the time," she tried to justify.

"Well, that's okay. I won't share it with her," he assured her. "As far as Nihal goes, he is a good guy, professionally as well as personally. A decent guy, comes from a good family, a little impulsive at times, but he means no harm to anyone." He was brief but that was enough for Rabani.

"Hmm," she said, weighing her words. "Is there any harm in meeting him again?"

"I don't want to influence you, Rabi. You are old enough to figure out what you are doing. But he is not a bad guy, that's all I can say."

"One more thing, Rabi," he continued after a pause, "You remember the guy from our flying academy whom Mannat hated the most?" he smiled.

"Yea, there was someone, I remember," she said. "Is it the same guy?"

He nodded as he heard Mannat call out, "Rabani, Neil, coffee is ready."

They both went into the living room. Rabani was sure about one thing, she couldn't discuss Nihal with Mannat. They kept talking about the next day's shopping plans and she just listened to them. Neil was leaving for Bangalore the next evening. She knew Mannat would go to the airport to see him off. 'That is when I could meet him,' she thought. But she couldn't help but wonder if it was indeed wise to meet him. Neil left for the night and both the sisters went up to their room after seeing him off.

They had a casual chit chat, mostly about Mannat's wedding preparations and the dress she was planning to wear. After sometime, Mannat dozed off, but sleep was far away from Rabani's eyes. She was still not sure about meeting Nihal again, while on the other hand, like Neil had said, there was no harm in meeting him. She could handle any situation, so she could handle this too, she thought. She reached out for her phone and checked his number. She wanted to text him, but then dropped the idea. She would do it in the morning, she told herself.

While Nihal and Rabani lay awake in their beds, sleep evaded Neil's eyes too. He too was worried. Both of them were dear to him and he couldn't see either of them upset. Moreover, Mannat and Nihal shared a completely different equation. He felt apprehensive about that too. He decided to speak to Nihal about this. He picked up his phone and texted Nihal to see him in the morning before he left for his jog, as it was really urgent.

Chapter 11

Come morning, the first thing Nihal did was to check his phone to see if there was any message from Rabani. There was one, but from Neil. He felt disappointed, yet tapped on it to read the message. He got ready and called him up to meet him in the park.

Nihal and Neil were sitting on a bench. Neil told him how he and Rabani were related and about the conversation he had had with Rabani the previous night.

"So, she is thinking about me," Nihal was happy to know, but the revelation that she was Mannat's sister pulled his spirits down. This was the last thing he had expected, that too when he thought that things between him and Rabani were working out for the better. "Why did you not tell me this before? I am sure you knew about it from day one."

"Because I didn't want to interfere, especially when I saw what a difference she made in your life. You were so happy and positive about her, I didn't want to ruin it by telling you that she is Mannat's sister. All I wanted was to let things take their own course. Moreover, I knew that if not otherwise, you would end up meeting her at my wedding anyway." He paused, "By the way, I did ask you to join us for dinner yesterday, and you only turned that down."

"Was she with you yesterday?" Nihal looked at Neil in disbelief.

"Nihal, she is a nice girl and if you are not serious about her, I would advise you to stay away. Now that you know she is family, you can understand how I feel about her."

Nihal threw his hands up in the air and got up from the bench. "Are you doubting me? Don't you already know how I feel about her? Do I need to justify it to you as well? Mannat seems to have a lot of influence on you. You've begun to speak like her now."

Neil pulled Nihal by his arm and made him sit again. "Don't get worked up. I have some good news too for you. She discussed it with me, so she is thinking about you as well," he paused. "She hasn't told Mannat and she won't, I am sure, as she thinks that her sister might overreact. Moreover, she asked me if she should meet you again, which means you still stand a chance."

"I know, I do," Nihal grinned and told Neil all about the episode that happened between him and Rabani.

"All the best, Nihal," Neil said. "But dare you do some nonsense, you will have to face me before anyone else. I never interfered between you and Mannat but with Rabani, it's different." He got up to leave, but then turned back to add, "Just a heads up, you are dealing with a DU gold medalist- a smart girl, but with a heart of gold." He left since he was getting late. Nihal kept sitting there for some time. Things were not as bad as they looked. She was thinking about meeting him. He checked his phone, but there was no message from Rabani still.

"Call up, please," he mumbled to himself.

Chapter 12

Nihal finished his breakfast, not taking his eyes off his phone. No call, no message. "Where are you, girl? Am I not going to see you again? Did you change your mind? No, you can't. You shouldn't, Rabani,' he was talking to himself. He got up and switched on the TV, but his mind was elsewhere. His father too asked him if all was well with him, as Nihal seemed quite lost. He nodded his head and started clearing the dining table. Just then, a message flashed on his screen.

"Hi, Rabani this side. Is this a good time to talk to you?"

"Hi, yeah, I am free," he replied.

The phone rang. He picked up call and went into the kitchen. "Hi, finally you called."

"Nihal, by any chance, would you be free in the evening today?"

"Of course, I am," he replied.

"Will it be possible to meet around 04:30 PM today? As I told you, I am going out with my family for shopping. Hopefully, we will be done by 4. Will it be possible for you to come to Ambience Mall, Vasant Kunj?" she said.

"I will be there, Rabani," he replied hurriedly as if she would change her mind if he didn't.

"If it's not a problem for you, we can meet at Starbucks," she suggested.

"Sure," he replied.

But I have a condition," she said.

'Condition!' he thought. But he didn't want to argue, "Whatever you say, Rabani. I am okay with everything."

"See you in the evening then," she said and disconnected the call.

Nihal was on cloud nine. Finally, she was meeting him.

In no time, his entire wardrobe, whatever he had there, was on his bed. Though he always looked nice in whatever he wore, he didn't want to take a chance that day. He called up Neil and said, "Try to wind up early. She is meeting me at 04:30 today. I don't want it to get delayed." Neil laughed and assured him of that. Nihal looked at his watch, "Oh, God! When will it be 04:30?"

Nihal reached Ambience Mall at 4 PM, since he didn't want to be late, and dropped a message to Rabani, "I have reached. You take your time." Neil had already hurried things up at his end. He ensured that everything was wrapped up by 4 PM, so that Rabani was free well in time. Rabani told everyone that she had to see an old college friend in the evening, so she would be staying back for some time. Neil and Rabani smiled at each other. Before leaving, Neil hugged her and wished her luck without anyone noticing it. He also warned her not to forget to meet him the next time she visited Bangalore and she promised that she wouldn't.

Rabani took a quick break in the rest room before meeting Nihal. She checked herself in the mirror, combed her hair and touched up her lipstick. She was all set to meet him.

Nihal's eyes were juggling between the entrance of Starbucks and his watch. "Come soon, girl. I can't wait to see you."

Sharp at 4.30, she was there. Nihal saw her coming; white long kurta and churidar, long hair and a beautiful smile. She looked amazing in her simplicity, he thought. He got up from his chair so that she could spot him. She walked in his direction and was in front of himin no time.

"Hello," was all that he could manage to say.

"Hope I am not late," she said and sat across from him.

"No, you are not. But what is your condition for meeting me?" he asked as soon as they settled down.

"Nothing much, but I would like to pay for my coffee. I don't like taking favours," she said firmly.

He started laughing, "See, I am a feminist to the core and it won't hurt my ego if you pay for my coffee too. I am okay with anything, as long as I get to sit with you," he replied.

She was perplexed at his wit.

"Okay, tell me something about you, Rabani. By the way you have a beautiful name."

"Thanks, but the credit goes to my grandfather who gave me this name," she paused. "There is nothing great about me. My name is Rabani and I come from a simple family. My dad is a retired army colonel and my mother- a home maker. I have an elder brother who is in England now and my elder sister Mannat was your batch mate. I have done my MBA in Human Resource and am currently working with a multinational HR company in Hyderabad. I am fond of reading, music and travelling, that you already know. I hope that is enough for now," she finished.

"Hmm, no, but that is not all. You haven't told me the most important thing about you."

"What is that?"

"You are beautiful, Rabani."

"You must be joking," she blushed. "The profession you come from has the best looking girls."

"Well, with no offence to anyone, all I can say is that they are smart."

"You mean that I am not smart?"She narrowed her eyes.

"I am literally struggling here to reason with you, which is good enough to prove that you are smart too."He got up from his chair. "I think I need some coffee since I've got to deal with a smart girl today."

She smiled and asked what he would prefer to have. They both went to the counter to place their order. He smiled as Rabani paid for the coffee.

"So, now your turn. Tell me something about you," she asked, settling down in her chair.

"Don't tell me you don't know anything about me, being Mannat's sister. In her eyes, I was the most despicable guy."

"You know, Nihal, we are raised in such a way so as to respect other's decisions, but at the same time, not get influenced by them. So, if I go by my sister's words, I shouldn't be sitting here at all. But you are not what she says or thinks about you, that's her opinion of you and I am sure you don't want me to go by her opinion."

Nihal was impressed as well as relieved.

He cleared his throat, "My name is Nihaljit Singh Bajwa and my story is even simpler. I don't have an impressive academic profile like yours, but like you, I too am into reading. It is more out of a requirement than a hobby really. My father is a retired professor and mother, a singer, but for the last few years, she hasn't been singing," he paused. The thought of what his parents were going through made him sad.

"And why is reading a requirement and not a hobby?" She asked, seeing him go quiet.

"I stay alone, so that's the best pass time for a lonely guy."

"Such a good looking guy and alone! What a waste!" Rabani teased him.

"What a pity!" Nihal laughed, "I hope I won't be alone anymore now."

Rabani blushed. "You said you wanted to tell me something. What is it?" She tried to change the topic.

Nihal thought of telling her about what he had been going through before he met her and what difference she had made in his life, but he didn't want to start with such a not-so-pleasant story. He dropped the idea. "I told you already, all I wanted to say was that you are beautiful."

"By the way, you didn't tell me a very important thing about you." Rabani tried to hide her embarrassment.

He frowned.

"You have a soulful voice and you sing so well, Nihal."

"Haha, so you were not sleeping that day, Rabani?"

Rabani was enjoying his company and was wondering why her sister had such a different opinion of him. "What is it between you and Mannat?"

He shook his head, "Nothing serious, actually. She is my friend, but she is different from others. We share a love-hate relationship. She thinks I am self obsessed. She had issues with me being too friendly with people." He paused, "She thinks I flirt with girls."

"And according to you, you don't?"She laughed.

"I do, if the girl is pretty,"he laughed too. "Your sister never likes to stand second, so we had a kind of a competition going on during our flying school days. But that is a thing of the past, and we are far ahead of thatnow, I think," he paused. "I haven't met her in a long time. You know, I am very close to Neil and she is the love of his life. I don't want any unpleasantness between them because of me, so I avoid meeting her. But now, I guess it's high time I should sort things out with her as she will be marrying Neil soon, and then we would be seeing each other often too."

She nodded in agreement.

"Thank you, Rabani.In spite of all that you've heard about me, you still agreed to meet me."

"I told you I don't go by others' opinions and besides, Neil told me that you are not a bad guy and I really value what he says."

They kept talking for a long time and Rabani found herself very comfortable in his presence. She looked at her watch. It was nearly 6.30.

"Don't tell me that you want to leave," he shrieked.

"Someone told me recently that Delhi is not a safe place for a girl travelling alone, that too in the late hours," she quoted him. They both started laughing.

"So, when are we meeting again? I owe you a coffee now," he said.

"Let's see," she replied.

"Do you want me to stalk you again?" He narrowed his eyes.

"I keep travelling to Bangalore so we may catch up sometime," she said.

"Riding a Royal Enfield? By the way, you look really hot riding that bike," he complimented her.

"Royal Enfield? How do you know about that?" she frowned.

"That is a secret," he rested his face in his palms.

"It belongs to my brother and I use it whenever I go to Bangalore. My brother was working there in Bangalore till a few years ago before leaving for England. After he left, I started using it but then, I too moved to Hyderabad. It's with my cousin now who lives in Bangalore," she explained. "But how do you know about it?"

"You see, my system works on coffee. Keep fuelling it and you'll keep getting the information. Now it all depends on when I get my fuel next," Nihal said.

She shook her head, "You are impossible!"

He laughed, "No, you give it a shot. I am possible."

They came out of the coffee house. Nihal called for a cab. "Let's go."

"Are you coming with me?" she asked.

"Yea, if that's not a problem. I stay that side of the city too, so will drop you home. Delhi is not safe, you see, and I will get to spend some more time with you."He made a cute face. "Rabani, I hope you enjoyed the coffee with me and it was not a total waste of your time and money."

She nodded.

"So, you don't mind meeting me again?"

"Why is it so important for you to meet me?"

"I will tell you when my system gets its fuel again," he grinned. "The next time, coffee is on me."He dropped her near her house and left.

Chapter 13

Rabani was in her bed, thinking about her meeting with Nihal - a good looking man with an equally good sense of humour, polite to the core and how could anyone miss his chivalry and good mannerisms. She thought about him, rather tried to find a flaw in him so that she had an excuse not to meet him again, but she couldn't find any. She could feel that she had already started liking him. 'That's not right, Rabani,' she told herself.

Mannat was busy sorting out her things in the room as their mother had told her to do away with the stuff that she wouldn't be requiring after her wedding. She was going through her cupboard and most of the things were scattered on the floor around her. Rabani got up and went to sit with her, so that she could think of something besides Nihal. She picked up an old photo album and started turning the pages. There were pictures from Mannat's flying academy days. She started scanning through the pictures and came across a group photo of her batch.

"You look so different here, Mannat."

"Is it?" Mannat joined her to peek into the album.

"Even Neil is looking so different here," she said, pointing at Neil. "Mannat, where is that guy you used to dislike the most?" She had brought up the topic purposely, so that she could find some grounds to dislike Nihal.

"Who? Nihal?" Mannat pointed to the person standing next to Neil.

Rabani looked at picture and said, "He looks nice."

"Yes, he was the best looking guy in our batch, so was very popular among the girls," she replied. "He is not that bad, Rabi. Those days, we were too young and he was my toughest contender. Moreover, Neil used to favour him a lot; that used to bug me even more. That was the reason I never liked him much," she explained. "Later on, when he came to know that Neil and I were seeing each other, he maintained a distance to avoid any unpleasantness between us. I haven't seen him for months, though he and Neil still are the best of friends and even stay together in Bangalore." Mannat stacked all the albums back in the cupboard.

"Hmm," Rabani nodded. She got up and went back to her bed. She had brought this up with Mannat so that at least her views about Nihal could help her change her mind. However, it seemed to Rabani as if the whole universe was in favour of him, for even Mannat didn't have anything to say that went against him.

Nihal reached home happy and excited, but his happiness was short lived. The family sat down to have dinner and he was busy talking to his father about Neil's forthcoming wedding. Suddenly, his plate went flying to the floor, "You both couldn't wait for Nihu to come back. I made this food for her," Neena screamed. By the time they realized it, half the things from the table were lying on the floor and Nihal's mother was trembling and crying.

"Oh, God! Not again," Nihal thought. She was having another fit of depression. He held his mother who was now crying inconsolably. Professor Nirmal rushed to call the doctor. In no time, the whole scene had changed. Their house regained that gloomy atmosphere once again that Nihal always hated. He wondered how his father must have been dealing with this all alone for the last two years.

The doctor arrived and attended to his mother while his father was trying to calm her down. Nihal stood dumb struck, watching all this helplessly. The excitement of that evening had died down somewhere within him. He felt as if nothing was ever going to change in his life. The dark memories of the past would always follow him wherever he went.

The doctor left after his mother felt a little better. She was given sedatives and was sleeping. Prof Nirmal cleaned up the clutter around the dining area. In spite of whatever had happened there that evening, he looked calm. He looked at Nihal as he went to help him, and asked if he was still hungry and wanted something to eat. 'How can he be so patient?' he thought and hugged his father. Tears rolled down his cheeks. He got up then and hurried to his room.

Nihal crashed on his bed as if no energy was left in him. 'Why can't I be happy in life? Why can't my family and I have a normal life like others? Is this going to go on forever? Will I ever get my once-so-loving mother back again?' His eyes welled up with tears again.

Prof Nirmal entered Nihal's room and called for him. Nihal wiped his face with the sheet on his bed and turned to look at his father. He sat down on one corner of his bed and asked when he was planning to leave for Bangalore. Nihal looked at his father who still looked very calm. 'How do you deal with all this all the time? Why don't you get her into a hospital? How long will you go on like this, papa?" he asked his father.

"Don't worry, Nihal.We are fine. Your Ma will be okay by morning. Don't think that I am doing some kind of a favour to your mother. She always stood by me through my thick and thin, then how can I leave her alone now, when it's my turn to stand by her? I have seen the best of times with her. You don't worry, everything will be alright. It's just a matter of time. This too shall pass. You don't understand the power of love. The day you find someone who would hold your hand throughout your life, it will all become very easy for you to understand. Life is not always as bad as it looks." Prof Nihal patted his back and got up to leave.

'He is so positive, even in such difficult times,' he wondered, admiring his father. 'The day you find someone...' his father's words echoed in his ears. He checked his mobile and opened the WhatsApp messenger. Rabani was online. He texted her to check if she was awake. She replied immediately.

"Thinking about me?"

"I was talking to Mannat,"

"About me?"

"You want me dead?" She joked.

"Yea, Ms. Sandhu Sr. can really do this," he replied.

"Why are you awake?"

"You want to know the truth, or am I allowed to lie?" He teased her.

"Truth and only truth," she said.

"I was thinking about you, Rabani. Thank you for coming to see me. Though you made me wait for nineteen long hours, it was worth it."

She texted back with a smiley.

"I am going back tomorrow," he told her.

"Via Hyderabad?"

"The Charminar is in Delhi these days, what will I do in Hyderabad?" He joked.

"You are really impossible, you know?" She texted.

"When are you coming to Bangalore?" Nihal asked.

"Not sure," she replied.

He sent her a sad emoji.

"Let's sleep now, Nihal," she said.

"I tried but I can't sleep. I wish I could get some more time with you," Nihal texted.

She didn't know what to say, so she didn't reply.

"Okay, Rabani, sleep now. It's really late", he texted when he didn't get a reply.

She sent a good night message.

He smiled and kept looking at her display picture till he fell asleep.

Chapter 14

Prof. Nirmal was right. Nihal's mother was okay by the next morning, though still weak and sleepy. Nihal woke up and went to see her. She was having breakfast in her bed. She smiled at him weakly and extended her hand towards him. He hugged her and kissed her head.

"Sorry," she whispered.

"It's alright Ma."

"I have made your lives hell," she looked at her husband.

"You know, Neena, you are such a wonderful wife. I can't imagine a life without you. Good or bad, heaven or hell, whatever it is, it's the best with you," Prof Nirmal tried to comfort her and it brought a child like smile to her face.

'Papa is matchless,' Nihal thought, looking at his father. "I wish, Rabani and I too could build such a bond.' He realized that he hadn't texted her since morning, so he got up and came to his room.

"Good morning, hope you slept well," Nihal texted.

"Yea, I did," Rabani lied. The fact was that she was up most of the night, just thinking about him. Flashes of instances from the evening before didn't let her sleep. She knew she was attracted to him.

“I am leaving this afternoon, how about you?” a message flashed on her screen.

“Tomorrow morning,” she replied and thought for a minute. “I am coming to Neil’s house to drop off a few things around 12 noon, will you be around?” She hadn’t wanted to tell him, but she couldn’t help it.

“I will see you there at 12,” he texted back.

'So, she wants to meet me again too.’ He looked at the clock, it was already 9. He showered, got ready and packed his bag. He quickly grabbed some breakfast and went to his parents’ room, so that he could spend some time with them before leaving.

Prof Nirmal was giving medicine to his wife. “There comes your son,” he said.

“I thought you left without meeting me, just like her,” Neena pointed towards the picture on the wall.

“No Ma, how can I? I never will. You know I never disobey you.” Nihal sat down next to her. She stroked his hair and kissed him. This was in a long time that his mother was showering her love on him.

“But now, you will be a good Ma. You will have your food and medicines on time and promise me that you won’t cry again,” he hugged her.

“I won’t,” she smiled. He spent some time with his parents and then left for Neil’s house.

Chapter 15

Nihal rang the door bell a couple of times. Neil's sister Ahana opened the door and said, "This could only be you, I knew."

He pulled her hair. In turn, she pushed him aside and they both ran to the living room.

Neil's mom, Raman, hugged Nihal. "You have forgotten your aunt. No one is bothered about this old woman anymore."

"How can I? By the way, which old woman are you talking about? You could still beat any of these Miss Worlds today."

Rabani stood up from her chair. "Oh! This is Mannat's sister, Rabani,"Raman introduced them. They smiled at each other.

Raman asked Ahana to arrange for some tea and started talking to Nihal, "Neil will be married soon, it's your turn next."

"Then you find a girl for me too. I will marry whoever you choose for me, but she should be as beautiful as you and should know how to bake those yummy cakes."

She laughed and got up to get some cakes for him. As soon as she left, he turned to Rabani and found her smiling at their conversation. "When will you stop looking so beautiful, Ms. Sandhu?"

She blushed and changed the topic, "You flirt with everyone, don't you? And then you blame my sister for accusing you a flirt."

He threw up his hands in the air, "No, I mean it. I am lucky to be surrounded by such pretty girls."

Rabani smiled and shook her head.

He laughed at her reaction. "How long will you take to finish? My flight is at 4 PM and if you'd be so kind to hurry up, I will get to spend some time with you."

"I am done here," she pointed at the packets she had brought to drop.

Raman and Ahana came back with tea. Rabani quickly finished her cup and got up to leave, saying that her mother was expecting her to be back for lunch. She signalled Nihal to check his phone.

"I'll wait for you outside the lane on the highway,"it read. In few minutes, Nihal left too, saying that he had to catch a flight to Bangalore soon.

Rabani was waiting for him in her car on the highway and started the engine as soon as she saw him coming.

"Where to?" He settled next to her in the car and pulled out her hair clip, making her hair fall loose over her shoulders. "Please, you've got such beautiful hair. Let people admire them."

She smiled and drove them to a café near the airport.

"You remember you've got to tell me something," she reminded him, settling down in one of the chairs.

"I have a condition. I will pay for the coffee today," he mocked.

"And for the eats too. I am very hungry, haven't had any breakfast. I went to sleep late and woke up late, then rushed to Neil's house," she said hurriedly.

"Anything to do with me?" He narrowed his eyes.

She shook her head and looked away, as if to hide how restless she had been since the moment she met him.

"Look at me, Rabani."

"What?" She looked at him.

"You sure, you slept well last night?"

She blushed and Nihal started smiling. He called for a waiter and asked him to get coffee and some snacks.

"I had seen you riding a Royal Enfield in Bangalore and was swept away. The memory is too pleasant to forget. Then, when I saw you at the Hyderabad Airport after almost two months, it took me no time to recognize you,"Nihal confessed when Rabani asked about the Royal Enfield again.

"You have a good memory."

"No, the girl is too pretty to forget."

Rabani laughed and shook her head.

"You don't believe me?"He opened his phone. "Okay, look at this." The wallpaper on his screen was a picture of her sleeping.

"Impossible!" Her jaw dropped. "You really are a stalker."

"There is something about you, Rabani. I could not forget you after seeing you that day in Bangalore. Though I knew nothing about you, I was sure that I will find you someday. You were always in my thoughts all through those days. That is the reason I was so informal with you when I met you on the plane for the first time. You were no stranger to me."

Rabani realized that she felt a connection with him too, though she didn't divulge it to Nihal.

They talked through the afternoon and didn't realize when it was time for him to leave. As they got up to leave, Nihal asked her if she could answer just one question. She agreed.

"Why did you tell me that you were coming to Neil's house?" He fixed his gaze on her face.

"Because you owed me a coffee." She looked away.

"I see," he said. "So it was just about the coffee; you didn't want to meet me."

She bobbed her head.

"Are you sure?"

"You said just one question," she reminded him cheekily.

He shook his head at her smartness. "Shall I expect a call from you whenever you are in Bangalore next?"

"Do I have a choice, Nihal?"

She dropped him at the airport and said, "Text me when you reach."

"I won't."

She looked at him in surprise.

"Why would I just text you when I know that I can hear you? I will call you, Rabani. May I?" He rested his elbows on the car window.

She nodded.

'Life has changed so much in the last two days,' Nihal thought. He had only expected her to take a step towards him, but she had been more than kind. She was not only meeting him, but also missing him and looking for ways to meet him again; defying her sister, making excuses at home, seeing him off at the airport and agreeing to meet him again in Bangalore. God was being too kind to him, he thought.

Whenever possible, he texted her or called her. Every time they talked, he found her to be equally excited to speak to him. He found her to be smart and witty, yet warm and caring at the same time. Life seemed to be back on track for Nihal.

Every time Rabani planned a trip to Bangalore, she made sure that Nihal was not flying that day. At times, they flew to Delhi together for weekend trips to their parents' places. He realized he was falling for hermore and more with each passing day. Though he never shared it with her, he was sure that she knew it too and felt the same way about him.

Not many people knew about these meetings, besides Neil and Barkat.

Chapter 16

Barkat was Rabani's cousin who stayed in Bangalore. They were of the same age and were the best of friends. They had shared all their secrets with each other since childhood. Barkat was about to finish her MS in Bangalore, and Rabani stayed with her whenever she was in Bangalore. Pillow talk was their favourite pass time, whenever Barkat didn't have a night duty. Those days, Nihal was their favourite topic for pillow talk. Only Barkat knew how Rabani truly felt about Nihal.

It was Barkat's birthday and Rabani happened to be in Bangalore. The girls planned to go out for dinner. Rabani invited Neil and Nihal as well.

"Another Ms. Sandhu!" Nihal pulled her leg over the phone when he heard about Barkat. "I don't mind as long as you are there, and I am being fed a yummy supper."

As planned, they went out for dinner. "What do you Sandhu girls eat?" Nihal teased the girls. "You are all so beautiful."

"Not just beautiful, smart too, you know. Though we don't come from a fancy profession as aviation," Barkat replied.

"Oh! I see, I am really popular among the Sandhu sisters." Nihal looked at Rabani, "Am I being discussed all the time?"

"Oh no, we have better things to talk about," Barkat retorted. Neil and Rabani enjoyed their conversation.

"Mannat was right," Rabani thought, "Nihal can make friends very easily. There is something about him that people get attracted to him so quickly."

Nihal and Barkat led the evening on, while Rabani and Neil simply enjoyed their arguments and remarks.

Back home, Barkat was all praises for Nihal. "He can make statues talk. No wonder, you couldn't resist him. He can make friends with anyone with the snap of his finger."

Rabani just smiled and listened to her.

Barkat was not wrong, Rabani thought. Whenever she met him, she noticed how friendly he was to whoever he met and interacted with. There was something about him that he couldn't be ignored. Probably that had been the reason why she couldn't ignore him as well, when he was trying to be friendly."

Rabani's head office was in Bangalore with a small unit in Hyderabad. She was leading a small team there, so she often had to travel to Bangalore for work. This gave her the opportunity to spend a lot of time with Nihal. Watching movies together and going out for dinners or disco became a thing of routine. At times, they ended up meeting some of Nihal's friends too, but he used to get rid of them quickly to be with Rabani again. "I told them that my friend has come from Delhi after a long time," he told Rabani at one such occasion.

"You shouldn't ignore your friends, Nihal."

"Haha, it's all worth it, Rabani.You won't understand," he laughed out.

At times, Barkat and Neil went along too, but he didn't mind them. Once, the four of them went to a pub and ended up meeting a bunch of girls who happened to be Nihal and Neil's colleagues. The girls asked them to join their group, but Neil politely turned down their offer.

After sometime, when Nihal went to get some drinks, one of the girls approached him. She chatted with him for a while. Nihal returned and told the three of them that the girls needed some help, so he would have to go with them, and asked Neil to drop Rabani and Barkat home. He whispered something to Neil before leaving, at which Neil smiled. Nihal left with the girls, leaving Rabani shocked.

"Two of the girls are really drunk, so they requested Nihal to help them get home," Neil informed Rabani. Rabani got a little upset. After sometime, she asked Neil to drop them home, as she had started to feel sleepy too. Back home, however, she kept thinking about the evening and Nihal's leaving with the girls in that manner did not go down her system well.

She started to relate it to the incidents when he avoided his friends for her. 'Maybe I too am just another friend for him now. He is surrounded by girls all the time. Maybe I too am just one such girl for him. Besides, he never said he loved me. He just said that he liked talking to me.' Her heart sank at these thoughts.

'I need to get hold of my emotions. If he thinks I am just a friend, I too should not think beyond that, or not reveal to him how I feel about him at least,' she thought.

Nihal tried calling her up late that night and then the next morning too, but she didn't take the call and just texted him that she was leaving for Hyderabad. Nihal didn't take it too seriously as she kept replying to his text messages and calls after that day too, but she tried not to sound too enthusiastic. When Nihal brought this up with her, she blamed it on work pressure. She reduced the frequency of her visits to Bangalore and sometimes didn't even inform him that she was in the city.

Nihal went to meet her in Hyderabad a couple of time too. She spent time with him, but tried to keep her emotions in check at the same time. Nihal sensed a change in her body language, but he believed her story of work pressure.

Barkat felt it too when during one of her trips to Bangalore, Rabani didn't inform Nihal about it. "Is everything alright between you two?" She asked Rabani.

"Yes, all good," Rabani replied without any enthusiasm.

"No, all is not good, Rabi. You've got to tell me what is bothering you."

"I am not sure if there is anything between us really. I like him a lot, but…" Rabani sounded low.

"Like him? I thought you loved him," Barkat shrieked.

Rabani kept quiet.

"As far as I can see, he loves you too, Rabi," Barkat tried to cheer her up.

"He never made any such claims. All he told me was that he liked to spend time with me. He says he finds me beautiful but then, he says that to every girl he meets; you, me, or his aunt," Rabani said in an irritated manner.

"So, Ms. Sandhu is jealous?" Barkat pulled her leg.

"I am not. It's just that I want to keep my emotions in check. I am attracted to him and if he doesn't share the same feelings as I do, then what is the point of dragging on this one sided thing and fooling myself? If he thinks I am just a friend, then I will only try to be that, and it's not necessary that I ought to inform him every time I am here in Bangalore."

"Rabi, I don't mean to interfere between you two, but I don't think there is any such thing. Whenever I've met him, with or without you, he doesn't talk of anything besides you," Barkat tried to appease her. "Still, if you want you can wait for some time, but I am sure you are taking him wrongly."

A few weeks passed by, and Rabani's changed behaviour started to bother Nihal. He asked Rabani about it a few times, but she made some excuse each time he asked.

"She is avoiding me, Neil," Nihal told his friend one day. "I fail to understand the reason. She has stopped calling me, just replies when I call. She didn't even inform me the last time she came to Bangalore."

"How do you know that?" Neil asked.

"I met Barkat yesterday. She told me that Rabani was in Bangalore the day before. I am losing my mind thinking of why she didn't inform me. Moreover, Barkat sounded quite strange too when she said that we are being stupid and wasting our time on silly things."

Neil was alarmed. "What exactly did she say?"

"I don't know," Nihal replied. "She asked why we were hiding our feelings from each other," he sounded disgusted.

"I don't really understand, what is there to tell? We both know how we feel about each other."

Neil looked at his face and then started laughing, "Wait a minute, you mean, you've never told her that you love her?"

"She knows," Nihal replied.

"That's okay, but did you tell her or not?" Neil asked.

Nihal shook his head, "No."

"Barkat is right, you are an idiot. You can sing for her. You can flirt with her. You can talk all sorts of nonsense with her, but you missed such an important thing. Even if she knows, as you think she does, is there any harm in expressing it?" Neil confronted him.

"No," Nihal shook his head.

"Then go and tell her, Nihal."

"But Barkat said that Rabani is in Delhi now."

"So?*Delhi kahan dur hai, bhai*. Go to Delhi." Neil patted his back. "By the way, I hope you remember it's her birthday this coming Friday."

"I know. I was planning to take off from work around her birthday," Nihal said unenthusiastically. "But now, she is there in Delhi. So what is the point?"

"Point is still the same. Don't change your plan. Just change the venue. Go see her in Delhi," Neil suggested. "Even I am going to Delhi on Friday."

Diwali was around the corner. Neil and Nihal had both thought of availing some leaves before the mad rush of Diwali started. Nihal was still not sure of how he would manage to see Rabani who was not even replying to his messages properly. But now, at least he knew what he was going to do as soon as he would meet her.

While Neil was grilling Nihal in Bangalore, Barkat was taking Rabani's case in Delhi. "You are an idiot, Rabi," she said. "If he is unable to express his feelings, why don't you try?"

"I don't even know if he loves me," said Rabani.

"Even a blind man can see that. Anyway, leave it. How about you, do you love him?" she confronted her. "Stop behaving like a typical girl and stop giving me this stereotype shit that it's a boy's job to make the first move."

"What if he says no?" Rabani didn't want to even think about it.

"Then I would say that he is stupid and it's better you stay away from him," Barkat replied sternly. "Give it a shot, Rabi.At least you would know which way to go. Don't assume things that are not true. He was stunned when he came to know that you were in Bangalore, but didn't meet him."

"What did he say?"Rabani asked.

"Nothing, he just seemed disappointed," Barkat replied.

Rabani started thinking about Nihal again, of how much she had missed him all those days. 'Barkat is right, I should tell him. Even if he doesn't think the same way about me, at least things would be more clear between us.'

Chapter 17

Colonel Dilraj Singh Sandhu was a retired army aviator. He lived in Delhi with his wife, Maninder, and daughter, Mannat. His son, Tejas, lived in England with his family. Rabani was their youngest child. Post retirement, Col. Sandhu had started working for social causes and was associated with an NGO that worked for the families of martyrs. He had lost many close associates during his years of service to wars and insurgencies, so he was well versed with the problems people faced after losing their near and dear ones.

His children had inherited the passion for flying from their father; Tejas and Mannat both were flyers. Both husband and wife had raised their children to be very independent, forthright and honest. There was a sense of mutual respect and love among them. Their children's opinions were heard and respected at home. Col. Sandhu was proud of his three children and their approach towards life.

Those days, they were busy with the preparations of the upcoming wedding of their daughter, Mannat, with Neil Singh Dhaliwal who happened to be the son of their long time friend and air force officer Wg. Cdr. Sukhwant Singh Dhaliwal. Neil had lost his father to a heart attack, when he was just 19. Col. Sandhu stood by his friend's family in those tough times and helped them sail through that difficult phase. Neil grew up to be a pilot. Neil and Mannat had been fond of each other right from their childhood days, when they used to accompany their fathers to the golf course. Raman and Maninder were the best of friends too. So, when Neil and Mannat told their families about their decision to get married to each other, both the families welcomed it.

Rabani was working on an assignment in Delhi, so she was staying with her parents those days. They were really thrilled to have her with them for some time. It had been long since she last stayed with them, though she visited them regularly, but those were short weekend trips only. Once in a while, her parents visited her in Hyderabad too, but then there is no place like home, so she was quite happy to be back in Delhi for a while too. Besides, she thought that as long as she'd be busy at home with her parents and sister, she wouldn't think too much about Nihal. But she was wrong; she couldn't stop thinking about him even for a minute. Moreover, Barkat's words kept echoing in her mind that she should express her feelings to Nihal, even if he was not taking that step. Such thoughts made her restless and she longed to see him.

Rabani was sleeping in her room when she was woken up by her parents and sister with a happy birthday song. It was her birthday, she realized. She was home on this day with her family after a very long time. She saw her parents, Mannat and Barkat standing there with a cake. Her brother, sister-in-law and nephew too were waiting to wish her on Skype. 'It is wonderful to have such a lovely family,' she thought. The cake was cut, the songs were sung and presents were given. She was showered with love and blessings. Amongst all this, she still missed Nihal and wished for him to be there too.

Throughout the day, she received many birthday messages from family and friends, but the one message that Rabani was waiting for never flashed on her mobile screen. She was disappointed. 'He doesn't even remember that it's my birthday.' The more she thought, the sadder she grew. 'Maybe he is done with me.'

There was a small get together at home that evening. Her mother always made it a point to make her children feel special on their special days. Unwillingly, she pulled herself up to be a part of the things going on at home. In the living room, her parents, Mannat, Barkat, Raman auntie and Ahana were present. Rabani's dad had taken out his Karaoke set and everyone was enjoying the music. Rabani remembered how as kids they used to have a lot of fun on such karaoke evenings at home with family and friends. But as they grew up and moved out of the house for work and other commitments, such evenings camp by only once in a while. Rabani tried to be a part of it too, to please the others and to divert her own thoughts from Nihal for some time.

It was Rabani's turn to sing. *"Tere bina, jiya jaye na,"* she started singing. Halfway through the song, someone covered her eyes from behind, but she still managed to finish the song. She knew it was Neil. As soon as she finished, Neil shouted, "Happy birthday, Sis-in-law! I have come all the way for you and you are not even looking at me."

She turned back and found Nihal standing there with Neil as well. He extended his hand to wish her. She was stunned. This was something she hadn't expected at all.

"How do you like the birthday gift?" Neil whispered.

Rabani managed a smile, still looking at Nihal.

Neil introduced Nihal to the rest of the Sandhu family as his and Mannat's friend who had come to meet Mannat. In no time, they were all a part of the celebrations.

Rabani tried not to look at Nihal, but her eyes were all out to defy her. Every time she looked at him, she found him looking at her. Though he was talking to Mannat and Ahana, his eyes followed Rabani all the time. Col. Sandhu offered him a drink but he politely refused, saying that it didn't go down well with his system.

When Nihal was asked to sing, he sang, *"Pal pal dil ke pass, tum rehti ho."*

'Once again, that heartwarming voice,' Rabani thought. Everyone at home enjoyed his singing. Col. Sandhu, being a big music fan, was particularly thrilled. Nihal had a natural charm that people couldn't ignore and the Sandhu family was no exception. At the dinner table too, he entertained everyone with stories about Neil, Mannat, and himself from their flying academy days. All this time too, however, his eyes followed Rabani wherever she went.

Post dinner, When Col. Sandhu asked for coffee, Nihal offered to make it, saying that he was very good at it. He asked for someone to help show him things around the kitchen. Mannat tried to get up, but Neil held her hand and asked Rabani to go with him. This was the moment that Nihal, Rabani, Barkat and Neil were waiting for.

Nihal followed Rabani into the kitchen. While she was taking out things from the cupboard, he went to stand behind her, so close that she could feel his breath. 'He is so close yet so far,' Rabani thought.

"Are you trying to avoid me, Rabi?"

"No," she whispered.

"Yes you are, and that too when I've realized that I am falling for you," he said.

"You are late Mr. Bajwa. I have already fallen for you first."

Nihal couldn't believe what he was hearing. "What did you say?"

"You need a heart to hear what I said, not just ears, Nihal," she replied. "Just like any other person around you, I too couldn't resist your charm and…"

"You are not just any other person in my life," he interrupted her.

They saw Mrs. Sandhu walking up to them so they changed the ongoing conversation and Nihal started talking to Mrs. Sandhu. "You have a beautiful family, auntie. I really enjoyed being here."

Mrs. Sandhu smiled at him, "Thank you, beta. If you really mean it, keep coming whenever you visit Delhi. I really love it when kids visit us. Else, it's just the two of us, waiting for all of you."

"Mom, you know it's only because of work. Otherwise, we all love to be here," Rabani said and hugged her mother.

"I surely will, auntie. Besides, who would mind such yummy food and the way you made all of us eat." Nihal thought about his own mother who once was exactly like Rabani's mom; loving and caring.

"Who all are there at your home?" Mrs. Sandhu asked casually.

"Ma and papa," he replied briefly.

"No plans of getting married? I am sure your parents too must be waiting for you to settle down," she asked.

Rabani rolled her eyes at her mother.

"Auntie, if you can find me a girl as beautiful as you, and one who can cook such yummy food, I would be ready to marry her right now," he said, pouring coffee into the mugs. Rabani shook her head. "Not again Nihal," she murmured and walked out of the kitchen.

While everyone was sipping their coffee, Nihal's mind was racing for how to be with Rabani alone. He knew that he wouldn't be at peace without talking to her. "I want to see you right now," he texted Rabani.

"Not possible, everyone is around," she replied.

"I don't care, I can ask for your mom's permission to take you out."

"You are not sane. Before my mom says anything, Mannat alone is going to kill you," she replied.

"I don't care about any of this," he texted again. "Please do something."

Rabani rolled her eyes in disagreement.

Nihal changed his strategy. He texted Barkat instead, "I want some time alone with Rabani and that too right now."

She nodded and messaged back, "Ask Neil to drop you at my place in an hour."

After everyone left, Barkat asked Rabani to come to her place for a sleep-over, as her mother was out of town. Since this was a regular practice at their place, Col. Sandhu easily agreed for it.

In an hour, Nihal was all set to be at Barkat's place with Rabani.

Chapter 18

Barkat had not told Rabani that Nihal was coming to see her. Rabani was depressed as she hadn't been able to speak to Nihal that evening. "Did you know that Nihal was coming for your birthday?" Barkat asked.

"No," Rabani shook her head. "We didn't speak all these days, so I didn't know. I thought he didn't even remember." She looked at Barkat. "Did you remind him about my birthday?"

"No," Barkat replied. "Why do you think he didn't remember your birthday?"

"Because there was no message from his side all day long. You know, today I really wanted to tell him how I feel about him, but everyone was around, so I didn't get a chance. We could hardly talk." Rabani rested her head on the back rest.

"There is always a next time," Barkat tried to cheer her up.

The door bell rang just then. Barkat asked Rabani to check who it was and went inside. In no time, Nihal was standing in front of her.

Nihal had waited for this moment for months and had rehearsed it many a times in his head for what he would say on such an occasion. But today, nothing seemed to be working. He kept looking at her as if trying to find the right words. "Rabi," finally, he said. "I don't know what to say and how to say it, but I have loved you since the time when you were not even aware of my existence. I have loved you since the day I first saw you in Hyderabad and you didn't even notice me. I wish I could make you understand what you mean to me and how you've changed my world. Since the day I saw you, I haven't been able to imagine my life without you."

Rabani was at a loss of words, so she started to look away.

He stepped forward and gently held her hands. "Look at me," he insisted. "Can't you see it in my eyes? I've never felt this for anyone."

Rabani couldn't say a word; she just rested her head against his chest and he enveloped his arms around her in turn. "It was really stupid on your part to avoid me."

"I was scared, what if you didn't think the way I do," she sobbed.

"You are right, Rabani. I don't feel the same way about you, as you do, because I don't know how you feel about me. In fact, you never told me how you feel about me, Rabi."

She looked up angrily. "I love you, Nihal."

"This is how you want to say it, rolling you eyes at me?" Nihal tried to cheer her up.

"I have always loved you. I loved you when you hummed that song for me on the plane. I loved you when you were stalking me. I loved you when you were mad at me for accusing you of being a stalker. I loved you when you said, you look beautiful, Ms. Sandhu. I loved you when you pulled out my hair clip." Rabani hid her face in his chest again.

" Just then? And all the other times?" Nihal teased her.

She hit him playfully in the chest. "What about you, Mr. Bajwa?"

"You mean the world to me, you silly. I love you to the moon and back," he said as he hugged her tightly. "Let me tell you one more thing, you look horrible when you cry; so horrible that I think I am falling for you all over again."

Nihal slid his hand into his pocket and pulled out a pendant, and tied it around Rabani's neck. "Happy birthday, Rabi," he whispered in her ear.

"You really remembered?" She said, surprised.

"No, not really. But I carry a dozen of these in my pocket all the time," he mocked, pointing towards the pendant. "So that whenever a girlfriend of mine has her birthday, I am ready."

She pushed him away, but Nihal held onto her. "You know, Rabani, I have a lock and since it's China-made, it's not very strong, but I bet you can't break it open," he said and enveloped his arms around her again. "Try if you can break it and set yourself free."

"I don't want to be free, Nihal."

"Done then, next time you try to run away from me, I will lock you right here," Nihal said.

"You are impossible," Rabani giggled.

"You try me, I am possible," Nihal replied.

They didn't realize, but it was almost 2AM in the morning by then. Nihal looked at his watch. "I should leave now. Extend my gratitude to Barkat; it couldn't have been possible without her." He then stepped out quickly.

"This was one of my best birthdays," Rabani thought.

She went to the bedroom and found Barkat already sleeping there. Rabani hugged her and said, "Thank you."

"You know, you shouldn't have let your Chinese lock go. He is so romantic," Barkat murmured.

"You peeping Tom!" Rabani pulled her ear.

Both the girls started laughing.

Chapter 19

It was a beautiful morning, more beautiful for Rabani after the events of the previous night. She was twiddling with the pendant that Nihal had given her. She was smiling, thinking about the night before. Nihal seemed to her like a character from one of those romantic novels that she used to read during her late teens - tall, handsome, though not so dark, but with a good sense of humor, wit, love, everything. "He is just perfect," she thought.

As soon as she returned home, a message flashed on her mobile screen. "Good morning, beautiful. What you are up to?"

"Nothing much, just missing you," Rabani replied.

"Oh! That means I need to do something so you don't miss me. Had breakfast?" he asked.

"Not yet," she replied.

"Want to have breakfast with me?" he asked.

"Yea," she smiled.

"Okay, your wish is my command," he replied.

"You are impossible, Nihal."

Rabani got up and went to the kitchen. Maninder was busy preparing breakfast. "I am making *aloo paranthas* for you all."

Rabani gently pushed her aside, "Let me make breakfast today."

"Are you sure, Rabi?"

"Yes," Rabani nodded and gently pushed her mother out of the kitchen.

After sometime, Barkat entered hurriedly and said, "Whose phone is this? It has been with me since last night. I took it with me by mistake. Similar phones, you know." She raised her hand to show hers'.

The door bell rang just then. This time, it was Nihal. "*Sat Sri Akal,* auntie," he greeted Maninder. "Sorry to bother you all so early in the morning. Have you found a spare mobile phone here by any chance? I have not been able to find mine since yesterday."

Rabani came out of the kitchen. "But you were..." She stopped mid-sentence as Barkat signalled her to keep quiet.

"Is this your phone?" Barkat asked Nihal.

"Yea, thank God," he replied. "I have been looking for it since morning."

Nihal, Barkat and Rabani smiled together.

Maninder asked Nihal to join them for breakfast. "Auntie, I have a weakness for food. I can't resist home cooked food, that too if mom makes it." Nihal coolly accepted the invitation.

Col. Sandhu asked him to sit next to him and the two got busy talking.

Barkat joined Rabani in the kitchen and told her how Nihal had asked her to cook up this phone story and had handed over his phone to her just before entering their house.

"He is impossible," Rabani shook her head.

"I know, that's why he loves you. No sane man can do that," Barkat winked at her.

Rabani nudged Barkat with her elbow and the two started laughing.

"These aloo paranthas are amazing, Rabani," Nihal complimented her. "I haven't had such tasty paranthas in a long time."

"Thank you, but I am sure your mum makes better paranthas. I am just an apprentice," Rabani replied. She tried to avoid making eye contact with him, so that no one would come to know that there was something going on between the two of them.

"Yes, she used to," he replied curtly.

"What do you mean?" Maninder asked.

"She doesn't keep too well, auntie. So doesn't cook nowadays. I really miss her food." His eyes reflected deep sadness

"We wish and pray that she gets well soon," Col. Sandhu tried to cheer him up.

"And you are most welcome to our place anytime," Maninder said warmly. Rabani had noticed the sadness in Nihal's eyes at the mention of his mother. 'Something is definitely bothering him," she thought.

Maninder asked the girls to get ready as they were to go to the Gurudwara that day. "Mannat has gone to pick up Neil."

"We are going to start with Mannat's wedding preparations today, so we plan to begin with a visit to the Gurudwara," she informed Nihal.

"Can I come along, auntie? I haven't been to a Gurudwara in a long time."

"Sure," Col. Sandhu replied. Meanwhile, Mannat and Neil reached home too and were surprised to find Nihal there.

"My phone, I forgot it here yesterday. It was with Barkat," Nihal explained to Neil, who smiled at Rabani in turn.

Col. Sandhu, Maninder, Neil and Mannat took one car, while Nihal, Barkat and Rabani took the other. As soon as they started, Nihal held Rabani's hand and said, "I don't want any confusion now. Before you have any more complains with me, I just want to say one thing."

"What?" Rabani looked at him.

"I love you," he winked. "And if you want, I can tell this to your mom, dad, sister, brother-in-law everyone, so that there is no confusion later on either."

"And what about me?" Barkat made a long face.

"Oh, you! You are the best thing that has happened to me after Rabani." They all shared a laugh as Nihal said that.

They went to Bangla Sahib. "You don't come to a Gurudwara often, Nihal?" Rabani asked.

He shook his head. "I didn't have a reason to come here for a long time. I used to think that He is not very kind to me." He paused as Rabani frowned at him. "Till I met you," he finished.

Rabani started smiling.

"Today, I have a reason to thank Him for giving me you. So I am here with you."

Before leaving, he told Maninder, "I am on leave till Wednesday. If there is anything I can do, please let me know. Mannat and Neil are my friends, I would be happy to be a part of their most special day." She smiled at him.

Rabani was happy to see her parents accepting Nihal's presence in their house.

For the next three days, Rabani spent most of her time either at work or with Nihal. "I am going to miss you once you go back after your leave," she told him.

"And I don't know how I will manage without seeing you all those days," he replied.

On the last day of his leave, Nihal asked Rabani to go shopping with him. "What are you planning to wear for Mannat's wedding?"

"Not sure, I have not decided yet."

"Come with me then. Let me take you out shopping," he insisted. Nihal made her try almost half the dresses in the store and shortlisted three out of them. "I want you to look the best among the Sandhu sisters," he said as he handed over his credit card at the counter for payment.

"I am okay as long as I look the best to you." She tucked his card back in his pocket and took out her own card to make the payment.

Obviously, Nihal was hurt. "Can't I buy you a dress?"

"You can, but when I ask you for one. Nihal, it takes a lot of effort to earn money and I don't want you wasting it on me like that. I don't even ask my dad for all these things now, since I have started earning," she said politely. "All I want from you is your love and affection. By the way, you brought this for me and I loved it." She reached her hand up to touch the pendant he had given her.

"You are beautiful in and out, Ms. Sandhu, and it's beyond my powers not to love you," he smiled. "May I?" He asked to carry the bags. Rabani laughed and handed over the load to him, including her handbag.

Nihal came to drop Rabani home. Maninder and Mannat were sitting in the living room. He pretended as if he had met Rabani just outside their house and was helping her in with the bags. "It seems you did a lot of shopping today," he said as he dropped the bags on the table.

"Yea, I went out for a meeting and ended up picking up some stuff afterwards," she replied, going through the bags. Maninder got up to make tea and Mannat started opening the packets. "They are beautiful, Rabani. Your taste has improved," she teased her sister, looking at the dresses.

"But looking at you and Neil, anyone can say that your taste is really good and his very poor," Nihal teased Mannat in turn.

Irritated, she threw a cushion in his direction, but he caught it while it was still in the air. Before Mannat could do or say more, Maninder was back with the tea.

"I am leaving tomorrow, auntie. If there is anything you want from Bangalore, please let me know," Nihal said.

"Ohh! But it was really nice having you here. We all hope to see you soon."

Nihal nodded looking at Rabani.

"Where in Delhi do you live, Nihal?" Maninder asked. "Your uncle and I were thinking of visiting your place to invite your parents to the wedding."

"It's not required auntie. Neil has already invited my parents. Neil is not just a friend, he is like a brother to me. We don't need an invitation for his wedding," Nihal said hurriedly.

Maninder nodded, "Okay, then. We hope to see you all at wedding."

After Nihal left, Mannat told her mother that though she didn't know all of it very well, but what she had heard from Neil was that all was not well at Nihal's place. His mother didn't keep too well and his father spent all his time looking after her.

Rabani was lost in her thoughts, 'That is why he never talks about his family.'

Chapter 20

Though Nihal had told Maninder that it was not necessary to send an invitation to his parents, Rabani wanted to invite his family personally to Mannat's wedding. Moreover, she wanted to meet his parents and see where he lived. So, she decided to visit his parents when he was not in Delhi. She had an idea that he and Neil were neighbours. So one morning, she found herself standing in front of his house.

Prof Nirmal was in the kitchen. His wife was sleeping after having had her breakfast and taking her medicine. She had been unwell for the past two-three days. To cheer her up, he was making *sarson ka saag*for her, when the door bell rang. He opened the door and found a girl standing there.

"Yes?" He asked.

"Are you Prof. Bajwa?" He nodded when Rabani asked.

"Uncle, I am Rabani, Nihal's friend and Mannat's sister," she introduced herself.

"But Nihal is in Bangalore."

"Yes uncle, I am aware. I have come to invite you and auntie to Mannat and Neil's wedding." She handed over the invitation card to him.

He looked at the card and then asked her to come inside. "Neil has already invited us," he said and asked her to sit.

"Yes uncle, but since the *sangeet* ceremony is going to be at our place, we wanted you and auntie to join us on that day too."

He smiled as he found her looking around, as if trying to find something. "What will you have, tea or coffee?" He asked and looked towards the bedroom, hoping that Neena wouldn't wake up.

"Whatever you prefer, uncle," Rabani replied. "But on one condition."

Prof. Nirmal looked at her inquisitively.

"I will make it," she said.

He smiled. "Okay, as you say. I will have tea." He pointed towards the kitchen.

Rabani followed him into the kitchen. She noticed the saag being cooked over the stove. "Where is auntie? Won't she have tea?"

"She is not well, so she is sleeping," Prof. Nirmal replied.

"Oh, are you making *Saag*?"

"Yea, I am trying to. My wife is fond of saag, so I am trying to cook some for her. You taste it and tell me how it is." He handed over a bowl and a spoon to her.

She tasted it and asked for some *makki ka atta* (corn flour) and a big ladle. She added the flour in and mixed it with the ladle.

"Let it cook for some more time," she said, sounding like an expert.

The tea was ready by then. She noticed Prof. Nirmal popping in a tablet with some water. "What was that for? It is completely safe to have that saag uncle," she smiled.

He smiled back, "Oh, this is nothing but old peoples' candies."

"But who is old here?" She mocked a frown and they both started laughing.

Rabani saw that it was a high blood pressure medicine that her mother had too.

Prof. Nirmal felt happy with Rabani's presence at their place. It had been a long time since their kids' friends visited them last. He looked towards the bedroom once again where his wife was sleeping, but she seemed to be sleeping peacefully.

"Who is she?" Rabani asked, pointing towards the girl in their family picture.

"She is Nihal's sister Niharika," he replied.

"I never knew Nihal had a sister.He never told me, I mean us," she fumbled.

Prof. Nirmal noticed it too. "Yes, she is Nihal's twin."

"Oh wow, that's amazing to have a twin," Rabani said excitingly.

"Yes," he nodded. He understood that Rabani knew nothing about it.

"Is she married, uncle?"

"Yes," he replied briefly. "What do you do?" Prof. Nirmal tried to change the course of their conversation.

"I work for a multinational HR company and am currently placed in Hyderabad."

"I have met Mannat once with Neil, but I never knew she has a sister too."

"Even Nihal didn't know," she said excitedly, but soon realized her mistake. "You teach Physics, right?"

"Yes, I used to, but now I am learning to make *sarson ka saag*," he joked.

"Nihal told us that auntie used to sing."

"Yes, she used to. Let me show you our music room," he said and got up from his chair.

He led her into a room which was both a music room as well as a library. There were books neatly shelved on one side, while musical instruments lay on the other side. "This is my study and Neena's music room," Prof Nirmal told Rabani.

"And who has won all these trophies?" She asked, pointing at the medals and trophies placed over a shelf'.

"Nihal and his mom, and a few belong to Niharika too. Did Nihal tell you that he too used to sing?"

"I heard him singing a few days back at our place." Rabani thought about the song that Nihal had sung on the plane. "He has a beautiful voice," Rabani went on, not realizing the sudden change of expressions on Prof Nirmal's face.

'Nihal has moved on for good,' he thought to himself.

Prof. Nirmal wanted Rabani to stay on for some more time, but feared his wife waking up, as he was not sure how she would react upon seeing Rabani in the house. So, when Rabani asked for his permission to leave, he didn't stop her.

"It was really nice to have you here, Rabani. I hope to see you again soon."

"The pleasure is mine, uncle. And yes, we are indeed meeting soon at Mannat and Neil's wedding," she reminded him.

"I can't promise it, *bitiya.* Nihal's mom doesn't keep too well these days. So we don't go out much. She doesn't like it and I too don't like to go out without her," he said sadly.

"Uncle, I think you should take her out. You never know, she might actually like it. It will be a nice change for her. Sitting at home all the time will only make her more sick."

"She won't. I know," he replied.

"Uncle, you are a physicist. Did you ever stop experimenting, thinking that you might not succeed? It may take some time for her to get out of the house, but then you should not stop trying." She paused for a minute as if thinking something. "You know, uncle, when I was a little girl, I once fell sick. The doctor prescribed a medicine for me, but it tasted very bad. I never liked to take it, but mom never stopped giving me that medicine. I used to trouble her a lot over it, but she used to make me have it by some or the other way. Slowly, I got used to the taste and started taking it without any fuss. And soon, I was alright," she smiled. "All I mean to say is, things will change only if we try to change them. If you try, I am sure it will work out for her and for both of you someday," she said.

Prof Nirmal marvelled at her wisdom. "I will try to get her to the wedding. At the very least, I will try to be there myself anyway."

Rabani left Prof. Nirmal with many questions, but he was relieved to know that his son had started enjoying his life again at least. He was making new friends and had started singing too. That evening, he insisted his wife to go out with him to a park nearby for an evening stroll. Though she didn't go that day, she promised that she would go out with him soon, and she did after a few days at his repeated insistence.

Rabani was really thrilled to meet Nihal's father too. Many times she thought of mentioning it to Nihal, but then convinced herself to wait till he returned to Delhi next. 'This way, I will get to see his reaction too.'

Chapter 21

Diwali was around the corner. Markets, houses 'and buildings were all lit up. Rabani felt especially happy as her brother Tejas was arriving that day with his wife Samaira and son Asis. Rabani was very close to her brother. If at all she had to share anything with any one, she would with Tejas. She was excited to meet her brother, but missed Nihalat the same time. "He is busy taking people to their homes, but what about me, his dad and his mom? It has been so many days since he left for Bangalore."

On Diwali morning, Nihal landed home. Prof. Nirmal was busy getting the house cleaned. Though they were not expecting any guests, it was more of a ritual at their place to clean up the house before Diwali. His wife had done it all her life, but since she got sick, he made it a point to continue doing everything the way it was done. When he saw Nihal walking in, he was elated. "I thought I would have to sit alone this Diwali too, like the last few years, but you've made my day."

Nihal hugged his father. "I have a day off, but I will leave by the mid-night flight."

"That's okay," he replied and hurried to the kitchen to check the breakfast preparations.

Nihal went to his mother's room and for a change; she was not on the bed but was sitting on a chair, watching TV. "You look much better today, Ma," he said and hugged his mother.

"Yes, I go out for walks now too."She kissed him.

"So the old man has finally started taking you out on a date once in a while."

"Not once in a while, he does it every day," she sounded excited. "You know, yesterday I had *gol-guppas* too."

"Not bad," Nihal smiled at his parents as Prof. Nirmal entered the room. They had their breakfast and Prof. Nirmal gave his wife her medicine. Both father and son came out of the room after putting her to sleep.

"I met Rabani." Prof Nirmal looked at Nihal.

"Who? How? I mean, where?" Nihal fumbled.

"She came home to invite me and your mother to Neil and her sister's wedding," he said calmly. "Sweet girl!"

"I told her not to visit you here," Nihal said. "Where was Ma? How did she react?"

"Your Ma was sleeping, she doesn't even know about it," he replied.

"Still, she shouldn't have come here," Nihal whispered.

"Apparently, Rabani doesn't know anything about Niharika or your mother's health, so you can't blame her."

"Was that not enough when I told her we don't need an invitation?" Nihal got up from his chair.

"Sit down, Nihal," Prof. Nirmal said firmly. "Why did you never tell me anything about Rabani?"

"There was nothing to tell, Papa. She is Mannat's sister. That's all."

"That's not all, Nihal, but I leave it up to you. Tell me whenever you want to. All I can say is that she is a nice girl: beautiful, smart, full of wisdom and cooks great *Saag* too. Tell her when you meet her next that I mentioned the *Saag* was really tasty." Prof. Nirmal tried to cheer Nihal up.

Nihal, though not very happy about it, was relieved at his father's reaction.

"Ms. Sandhu, you are impossible," he mumbled and picked up his phone. "Where are you?" he texted Rabani.

"Where are you? No news since last night," she replied.

"Can you meet me for lunch? I have got to leave for Bangalore tonight," he texted back.

"Are you in Delhi?" She was excited.

"Yea, but won't come to your place," he replied. "See you at 1.30 at the café."

At 01:30, Rabani was sitting in front of Nihal. "My brother and his family reached just this morning, but I couldn't miss meeting you. They will be here for a month."

"Your parents must be thrilled," Nihal said. Before she could reply, he asked, "You visited my parents?"

"Yep, and you never told me that you have such a loving father and a twin sister. I couldn't meet your mom, she was sleeping," Rabani went on.

"Why? I told you I don't need an invitation," he cut her short.

"Yea, but..." Rabani tried to speak.

"That too without informing me and in my absence?"

Rabani was taken aback. All she could say was sorry, though she wanted to say much more. She had not expected such a reaction from Nihal. The excitement of seeing him died down. "You wanted to meet me just to ask this?"

"If I asked you not to come to my place, there must be some reason behind it. Don't you get that?" he yelled.

"Had I known you won't like it, I wouldn't have done that," she replied meekly. Her eyes were swimming.

She quickly finished her coffee and got up to leave, as she didn't want to cry in front of him.

"Wait, I will drop you home," he got up hurriedly, leaving some bills on the table, but she was gone.

Rabani was still trying to figure out her mistake. Tears rolled down her cheeks. She thought Nihal would be surprised, if not thrilled, but this reaction of his was the last thing she had expected. She reached home and locked herself in her room, saying that she had a headache.

Nihal kept sitting in the car for some time. He too was upset with the way he had behaved. "She had been waiting for me all these days and this is how I behaved," he felt guilty. "Papa was right, she knows nothing. All she wanted was to make me feel special." He started his car and drove to Rabani's house.

Everyone was sitting in the drawing room, he saw as he entered. Col. Sandhu introduced him to Rabani's brother and sister-in-law. He greeted everyone but Rabani was not there. Casually, he asked about her and Mannat, if the girls were working on Diwali too. He was told that Mannat had gone to meet Neil's mother and Rabani was not feeling too well and was sleeping in her room. He didn't know what to do.

Nihal texted her, though he didn't expect a reply, "I am sitting with your dad in the living room. I am sorry, Rabani. I didn't mean to hurt you. Will I get to see you before I leave?"

"Give me a minute," she replied immediately. Nihal was relieved.

Rabani got up from the bed and looked in the mirror. Her eyes were swollen red and she looked horrible. 'I can't go out like this.'

Quickly, she washed her face, adjusted her clothes and went to the living room. Nihal was talking to her brother, Tejas. Rabani went to sit next to Tejas. He hugged her and asked her how she felt.

"I am okay, Veerji, just a seasonal cold. I should be fine by evening." She looked at Nihal who was looking at her with an apologetic look on his face. He looked upset. She smiled at him weakly.

After a while, she addressed Nihal, "The pen drive you gave me is password protected, so I couldn't copy the contents."

"Is it?" he replied. "Let me see," he was happy to get a minute alone with her.

"What pen drive?" Col. Sandhu enquired.

"Dad, he got some new Karaoke versions of songs for you," Rabani replied and asked Nihal to come with her.

She took him to her room. As they entered the room, Nihal held her hand.

She turned around to face him. "I am sorry, Nihal. I didn't mean to offend you."

Nihal was surprised. He had expected her to be mad at him. "I am sorry, you silly. I was rude and unreasonable. Why are you being sorry?"

"I should have listened to you when you said that none of us should go to your place. I should have understood that there must be some reason behind what you said."Tears rolled down her cheeks again.

"It's okay. You didn't know since I never told you anything about it. Believe me, let this wedding thing be over, I will tell you everything honestly about me and my family," he assured her. "You know, Papa really liked you being there and asked me to convey to you that your *sarson da saag* was very tasty," he said and hugged her. "I don't know if I will ever be able to understand you. You are impossible. I was thinking that you must be upset with me, will shout at me and won't talk to me, and here you are blaming yourself for everything."

"I don't like to waste time fighting. Remember, you once told me that you never meant me any harm? I believe that. Moreover, your Chinese lock doesn't let me go away from you," Rabani said softly.

"You are so cute, Rabi." He wiped her face and hugged her again.

"What is going on, guys?"A voice jolted Rabani and Nihal out of their embrace. Rabani's sister-in-law, Samaira, was looking at them in dismay. Nihal released Rabani from his arms.

"I can see another love story in the making," she said and twisted Rabani's ear. "Since when have you both been fooling everyone here?" she laughed and asked in a low tone. "Careful guys, *deewaron ke bhi kaan hote hain.* Quickly finish your Diwali greetings before anyone else sees you. I shall go back and join everyone," she said and left. Rabani and Nihal followed her out.

Nihal came back home and spent the evening with his parents. After many years, Diwali had a different feel at the Bajwa House. Though there were no celebrations, yet Nihal and his parents were at least together and talking about something besides their gloomy sad past.

Chapter 22

Mannat and Neil's wedding celebrations were on, both at the Sandhu as well as the Dhaliwal residence. The Sandhus' house was full of guests. Nihal too had taken some time off from flying. He was shuttling between the Sandhu and Dhaliwal household. Thanks to Barkat and Samaira, he got to spend a lot of time with Rabani whenever he was at her house. The only person still not very happy with Nihal's presence was Mannat. So, Nihal thought it was high time he should sort things out with Mannat.

"You should be at Neil's house, as you are his guest," Mannat told him one afternoon.

"Who said that? Your parents have sent me an invitation too," he said cheekily.

"The invitation is for the wedding, not for flirting with my sister and cousins."

"You Sandhu sisters are so pretty, who can resist flirting with you all. But I am not flirting here, I mean this very genuinely. You girls are amazing, beautiful, smart, independent, well mannered and down to earth too.

Mannat softened a bit. He held her hand and made her sit on the sofa, then sat next to her. "You know, Neil is really fortunate to have you. I am sure that you will bring him happiness in life with your love and care. After his dad's demise, he and Raman auntie have been through a lot. Ahana was too young to understand anything. You know all this better than I do. Neil and I have been like brothers and if you say anything against me, he won't like it. You and I have had our issues, and we were quite immature at that time, but we are grown up now and can handle things better. Still, if you are not comfortable with my presence in his life, I will distance myself from him, but I know he won't let me do it." Nihal's eyes grew moist with these words.

"You know, you are not as horrible as you look. So the bottom line is, I either upset Neil or tolerate you for the rest of my life. I choose the latter," Mannat patted his hand. "You are right, we were kids at that time and fighting with you was a part of growing up, but I never hated you, though you were very irritating." She sighed, "When your friend proposed to me, he told me clearly that I will have to accept you with him. I love him, so I had no choice."

Nihal hugged her.

"But you will stop flirting with my sisters," she warned.

"Never in my life," Nihal smiled.

It was the Sangeet night. Rabani was wearing the off-white and magenta *ghagra-choli* that Nihal had picked up for her.

"You look beautiful, Rabi," Samaira complimented her and joked with her mother-in-law that they should start looking for a suitable groom for Rabani too, unless she liked someone.

Rabani rolled her eyes at her, and Samaira and Maninder laughed together. "I think so too. I have a few suitable prospects in my mind," Maninder said

"Mom," Rabani retorted. "You both have better things to do at the moment. We are going to have guests soon." Maninder walked out hurriedly at these words.

Barkat came in just then and said, "Guests have started to arrive and there is this one guy, wearing a turban, who looks irresistibly hot." *'Pagg wala munda bada sohna lagda'* she teased Rabani. However, Rabani didn't know who she was talking about.

Nihal was standing in the doorway, wearing a black *Pathani* suit, an aqua blue waistcoat and a blue turban. Rabani's heart skipped a beat. She had never seen him in a turban. 'Barkat was right, he looks adorable.'

"You are looking beautiful, Ms. Sandhu. I can't keep my eyes off of you," he complimented.

Maninder came back inside to take her purse. "Look at my son, you look so handsome," she hugged Nihal.

"I am no match to your grace, auntie," he replied.

Barkat and Rabani shook their heads. "You are impossible, Nihal," Rabani whispered and the girls giggled.

The evening was full of fun and frolic. Amongst everything, Nihal tried to spend as much time as possible with Rabani. His sweet nothings made her smile and blush at the same time, making her look even more beautiful. He made sure that everything was done in the best possible way from the groom's side. Mrs. Dhaliwal depended completely on him for everything. He made sure that Ahana was never left unguarded in the crowd while dancing. "See, he is a responsible man," Neil whispered to Mannat.

"We were expecting your parents too," Maninder said to Nihal.

"Mom is unwell," he gave the usual reply.

Maninder looked worried, but Nihal assured her not to worry and that his mom would be fine soon. Maninder was thinking of meeting with Nihal's parents, having seen the closeness between him and Rabani. She had noticed the fondness in their eyes for each other too. She and Col. Sandhu liked Nihal. Within a few days, he had become an integral part of their family. Moreover, Neil and Mrs. Dhaliwal held a very high opinion of Nihal and his family. She made a mental note of dealing with this later and got back to the proceedings of the evening.

Nihal was a brilliant singer; everyone enjoyed his songs and *boliyan*. He was appreciated by all. "All these aunties are eyeing you for their daughters," Barkat teased Nihal.

"I hope the right auntie thinks so too, Barkat."

Rabani heard this and joined them. "Oh! My mum?" She stopped and blushed as she realized what she was about to say. Barkat started laughing, but Nihal felt sad.

'We both love each other so much and want to spend our lives together. Rabani must have dreamt big about her life with me, but will that ever be possible? Will she ever be happy with me in that house? She deserves all the happiness in life, but what will she get at my place?' he thought.

After the Sangeet when everyone had left, Maninder was sitting in the living room with Mannat and Samaira. They were talking about how well the function went and that everyone had a great time.

"I was expecting Nihal's parents to be there today, but they didn't come," Maninder said, disappointed.

"I thought so too," said Samaira.

"They won't, mom," Mannat replied. "Nihal's mother is sick, so they don't go anywhere. Neil told me that Nihal's mother has not been very stable mentally since her daughter's death. She is not even told that Neil and I are getting married."

"Oh," said Maninder and got lost in her thoughts.

The Sandhus and the Dhaliwals had planned the wedding to be a quiet family affair, followed by a grand reception. As decided, the wedding ceremony was held in the Gurudwara, where Mannat and Neil took their vows to spend the rest of their lives together in the presence of *Waheguru* and their families.

Chapter 23

The reception venue was full of guests. Friends and family had gathered to extend their wishes and blessings to the newly married couple. Among all the guests, there was a man whom no one had expected to be there. Prof. Nirmal, after ages, had come to attend a wedding reception. For the last two years, all his outings only consisted of visits to the doctors, the pharmacy or the grocery store. Once in a while, he would visit some relative if it was a very serious or urgent affair and if he could make some suitable arrangement for his wife in his absence.

Neil got up from his chair as soon as he spotted Prof. Nirmal and rushed down the stairs to hold his hand. "I am so happy to see you here, uncle. It's the best gift I've received for my wedding."

He hugged Neil in turn and wished him and Mannat a happy married life.

Mrs. Dhaliwal too was very happy and got emotional to see their old friend around. "I am so grateful that you are here to bless Neil and Mannat. I wish Neena too were here."

"I will surely get her someday," he replied.

Nihal too was surprised to see him there. "Papa, where is Ma?"

"She is sleeping. A servant is there with her," he replied.

He was then introduced to Col. Sandhu's family. "We have known Nihal for quite some time now, but never got to meet you. We feel honored that you could make it here today. Neil and Mannat are going to start a life together and it's nice of you to grace the occasion and bless them with your presence," Col. Sandhu said politely.

Almost everyone was there, but the one person whom Prof. Nirmal had come all the way for was not to be seen. Rabani had hid herself somewhere, thinking that Nihal would be annoyed if he saw her with his father again. Prof. Nirmal looked around but couldn't find her. He wanted to ask Nihal, but kept quiet thinking that perhaps Nihal didn't want him to meet her again or perhaps there might be nothing between them and he was just thinking too much. He sat down and looked around for Rabani, but she didn't come to meet him. He had whatever little he wanted to eat just to stay there for a little longer, but he couldn't meet Rabani. Disappointed, he got up from his chair to leave. Nihal offered Prof. Nirmal to drop him to his car, but he refused saying that he was required at the venue more. "I'll leave now. Your mum might have woken up."

Prof. Nirmal sat down in his car and turned on the ignition. He then turned around in his seat to see if the way was clear to reverse the car out, and found Rabani sitting in a car right behind his, all alone. He stopped, got down and walked over to her.

She got out of the car on seeing him too. "*Sat Sri Akal,* uncle."

"Where have you been and what are you doing here? I have been looking for you the entire time," he asked with authority.

"I had come to get a few things from the car, uncle," she lied.

"Are you sure that you are not trying to avoid me?" he asked.

"No, uncle. Why would I try to avoid you?" she lied again. "Nihal didn't come to see you off?"

"How do you know if I am coming in or going back?"He folded his arms and looked straight into her eyes.

"I am happy you came here. How's auntie?" She tried to smile, looking all around to check if Nihal was nearby too.

"I came all the way to meet you, *bitiya*, but my *bitiya* doesn't want to meet me."

Rabani ignored what he said. "Did you have food?"

"Hmm," he nodded. He noticed that Rabani was looking around nervously. He opened his car's door and asked her to sit inside. She did as she was told. Prof. Nirmal sat inside too.

"Are you scared of Nihal?" he asked.

"No," she shook her head.

"I came all the way to tell you that this physicist has not stopped to experiment. My being here itself speaks that I am giving life another chance. Hopefully, things will fall into place bit by bit, as you said," he said.

Rabani smiled.

“Now you look like the girl I met at my house," he smiled back. “My son needs someone to hold his hand in his good times and bad, through his ups and downs, his thick and thin. I see that in you, Rabani. Hold him when he is low or weak. It’s just a difficult phase and shall pass soon. All you need to do is to be a bit patient with him, and I know you can do it.” He paused. “If you want, don’t tell him that you met me. I won’t tell him either.”

She nodded. “Thank you, uncle. You came all the way just to meet me.”

“No no, it’s not just you. I got bored of that boring self-cooked food every day, and after that saag the other day, I really wanted to have something as yummy as that again.”They both shared a laugh. “God bless you.”

“I should go now, else your son will find out our little secret.” She stepped out of the car and Prof. Nirmal left for his home.

Rabani entered the venue and found Nihal looking for her. He pulled her to a corner and said, “Papa was here.”

“Oh," she looked around amused.

“He just left, a few minutes ago. Where were you? I wanted you to meet him.”

“Hmm…I had gone to see off a friend," she said carelessly, as if she didn’t understand what he was saying.

“You don’t look very happy or excited," Nihal complained.

“Yea, I am happy for you and him.”She was trying her best to sound indifferent, so that he wouldn't come to know anything.

"I wish you had been here," Nihal said.

"What is the point? You didn't want me to meet your family, so I avoided being around when he arrived. I knew your papa was here, Nihal."

Nihal looked at her in surprise.

"Your reactions are so unpredictable at times, so I thought it was better to stay away," she said bluntly.

"You are still upset about that day," he said apologetically.

"No, Nihal. I am not, but I didn't want to spoil both our moods again, today of all days at least. He hardly knows me. For him, I am just another girl, Mannat's sister and Neil's sister-in-law, so it's not important if I am introduced to him or not. Besides, I don't want to annoy you."She tried to keep a straight face. "Now please excuse me, I have other things to do and so much to deal with."

Nihal stopped her, "What is it that you are going to deal with?"

"Nothing, my mum is at the best of her moods, the mommy mood, you know. Mannat is leaving today, so you can imagine what my mom is going through."

"That happens with every mother whose daughter is leaving," Nihal replied.

"Hmm," she said with tears threatening to drop from her eyes.

"And this is how you are going to deal with it?" he frowned, pointing at her tears. "Let me handle it, you don't worry. Your mom will be fine but first, you give me that vibrant smile."

Rabani smiled, holding back her tears.

"That's like my Rabi," Nihal smiled back.

When it was time for Mannat to leave, as Rabani had predicted, Maninder was crying inconsolably, hugging Mannat. Nihal held her hand and asked her to sit in the car with Mannat. She looked at him surprised.

"You are coming with Mannat, she is not ready to leave without you either," he explained.

"No, I can't," Maninder sobbed.

"Why?" Nihal asked.

"I can't go with her. She has to live her own life and make her own decisions from now onwards. No mother goes with her daughter after the wedding."

"When you already know all this, why are you not sending her away happily? You want her to carry with her memories of you being sad and upset?" he asked.

Maninder's sobbing stopped and she started smiling. He hugged her and assured her. "Mannat will not have any problems there. Neil is best of all men I know and as for Raman auntie, you know her better than I do. See your daughter off with your best smile that she will cherish all her life," he said and handed her hand to Col. Sandhu.

Col. Sandhu patted his shoulder. Rabani, Samaira, and Tejas smiled at Nihal too.

Nihal took the driver's seat and started the engine. "Thank you," Mannat gently patted Nihal's shoulder from the rear seat. "I was worried about my mum the most." He smiled in return and in no time, Mannat was at Neil's house.

Chapter 24

Most of the guests left soon after the wedding. Tejas and Samaira returned to England with their son too. Before leaving, Tejas made his parents promise him that they would visit him and stay with his family for at least a few months every year. "I didn't insist earlier because Mannat was there with you. But now she is settled and Rabi is in Hyderabad too, so you have no excuses left. I have asked Rabi too to look for a job in England and move there with us. England has so much better opportunities for her. Even her current firm has a nodal office there. We want to spend some time with you all and little As is deserve to be with his grandparents too," he said, pointing towards his son. Col. Sandhu promised him that he would consider his proposal seriously.

Rabani returned to Hyderabad after finishing her assignment in Delhi. Nihal moved out of his apartment to make way for Mannat and rented a studio apartment instead in the same building where Barkat lived. Mannat switched her job and shifted to Bangalore with Neil. Mrs. Dhaliwal decided to move to Bangalore too after Ahana finished her twelfth grade in Delhi. Things seemed to be working out for everyone.

While everyone was busy in their respective lives, Col. Sandhu and Maninder got a new job to do too. During Mannat's wedding, Prakash and Pritam had visited them with their daughter Resham and her five year old son, Bunny. Pritam and his wife Prakash were the caretakers of Col. Sandhu's farms in a village near Hoshiarpur. A few years back, they had married their daughter Resham off to a boy from the next village. But her husband died in an accident when Bunny was just three years old. Resham's in-laws disowned her and her son, so she came back to her parents.

When Col. Sandhu heard about this, he decided to do something for her. He and his wife thought of getting her to Delhi and making her finish her studies, so that she could fend for herself and her son. They got her enrolled in an open school to appear for class 12th exams and Col. Sandhu arranged for her coaching too. After the wedding when everyone left, she stayed back with the Sandhu couple and started preparing for her exams. So, Col. Sandhu postponed his England plans for a few months.

Nihal and Rabani were busy in their own small world, spending as much time as possible with each other. Whenever Nihal had an off, he went to Hyderabad and whenever she was in Bangalore, she spent all her time with Nihal after work.

At times, Barkat joined them too. Rabani found him to be very patient and a hassle free man who didn't get mad at people for little things. His wit and sense of humor was extraordinary. Life seemed to be fun with Nihal around.

Nihal discovered Rabani to be a very sensible and caring girl. Though a tough task master at work, she was an easy going person at home, who didn't waste her time finding faults with others. With her love and care, Nihal seemed to be getting over his past.

New Year's Eve was approaching. It is the time when most people plan to have a vacation but by virtue of his profession, Nihal was busier than ever. "Festival and vacation times are the busiest for a flyer," he told Rabani. "You've got to learn to live with it. I would be flying on Christmas as well as New Year's Eve. You better plan a vacation with your friends."

"I would better sit down and work in my office," she made a sad face. As he had told her, he was really busy during the New Year's time.

On the contrary, Barkat had her vacations then. Her MS had finished, so she had planned to go to Cochin with her friends. "Why don't you join us, Rabi?" she asked.

Initially, Rabani refused but then some meeting came up in Cochin from her office side. Since no one from office was willing to go during the festival time and Nihal was busy anyway, she decided to go to Cochin.

"I am happy that you are finally going out. I was worried that you would sit at home and sulk about being alone," he said, after she told him her plans.

He sent her a beautiful dress, saying, "Wear this for the New Year Eve party. It will make you look even more beautiful."

"What is the point when you are not even there to see me wearing it?" She made a long face.

As planned, Rabani joined Barkat and her friends in Cochin. The gang was busy sightseeing and shopping in the city. Rabani seemed to be enjoying the trip, but she longed for Nihal's company. Nihal kept calling and texting her whenever he got the time and tried to cheer her up.

On New Year's Eve, there was a gala dinner in the hotel courtyard. The girls decided to rock the evening and pulled Rabani along too. Rabani wore the dress Nihal had sent her. It was a beautiful backless lilac coloured dress with purple and pink flowers on it. He was right; she looked more beautiful than ever in that dress. Before leaving for the party, Rabani tried Nihal's number but his phone was not reachable.' He must be flying.'

While at the party too, she tried his number a couple of times, but it was still switched off. When Barkat caught her staring at her phone, she snatched it, tucked it away in her pocket and pulled her to the dance floor. She danced for a while, but went sit down again. After sometime, Barkat came running to tell her that Nihal had called and that he said he would call back in half an hour. "So, you will get your phone back after half an hour, but only if you behave like a good gal till then."

Rabani joined her back on the dance floor. Barkat got drinks for everyone, while Rabani just tried to get along with the gang.

Half an hour passed, but Barkat had now vanished. Rabani's patience was wearing out. When she finally saw Barkat coming in from outside, she yelled, "Do you realize it has already been half an hour and you vanished with my phone. Nihal must be waiting for the call."

"See, there is no call from Nihal," he said as she handed her the phone.

Rabani didn't wait to look at the screen. She snatched her phone back and rushed back to her room, as it was too noisy outside. She wanted to speak to Nihal before he slept.

Chapter 25

Rabani unlocked her room, entered and reached to drop the key-card in the slot, but there was already a card in the slot. Before she could understand anything, a strong hand slid around her back and held her. She tried to scream, but another hand gagged her mouth. She tried to resist out of the hold, but it was so strong that she couldn't move an inch. A pair of lips touched the nape of her neck softly, though the grip of the hands was still very hard. It was too dark in the room for her to see anything. All she could feel were two strong hands gripping her and a pair of moist lips gliding down her neck to her collar bone. She knew she was in trouble. She struggled to get free, but all was in vain.

The hand on her back swirled her around and she felt a strong masculine bare chest against her relatively soft body. Both her hands were held tightly behind her back now and the pair of lips now perched over hers. She felt shivers running down her spine. A strong masculine smell numbed her senses. One hand took charge of both of hers, while the other moved freely up to her face, then gently slid down to her neck and pulled her hair clip out. Her hair fell loose across her face.

"Nihal!" she screamed.

"Happy New Year, Ms. Sandhu," she heard.

Blood started to flow in her veins again as she recognised those lips and that familiar masculine odour.

The grip of his hands loosened, but Rabani held on to him tightly, nibbling at his chest, his neck and lips. She touched his lips softly with hers and opened her mouth as they kissed. Those hands moved over her back again and she shivered, but ecstatically this time. His lips moved down to her neck again. She moaned feebly. The pair of hands unzipped her dress and it slid down her waist to the floor.

Those hands pressed her soft body against his firm frame. She felt her orbs against his firm toned body, and it felt heavenly. There was something magical in his touch when he gently held those mounds. She was going weak in her knees, so she left herself loose in his arms. She was in two strong arms and was being carried to the bed. She was clinging on to him and didn't leave him when he put her to bed. He cupped her firm orbs and gently stroked the nipples; they were hard. It sent shivers down her spine.

She moaned lightly and whispered in his ears, "I love you, Nihal," and bit his ear lobes passionately.

In turn, he bit her nips. It was painful yet pleasurable, she thought. The pair of lips wanted to cover every inch of her soft milky body. With the hands still holding the mounds, the lips carried on their downward journey. Every inch of her body was burning with desire. He touched her naval and dived his tongue in there. She cried and tugged at his hair tightly. He kissed her belly button. His hands slid down between her legs and stroked her thighs. He pushed her panties aside and dived his finger inside her. It was warm and moist. He waited and then pulled out after a minute. She yelped.

He tried to get up, but Rabani clutched his hand and guided it back between her legs. Emotions were running high. She rose, resting on her elbows and pulled him closer. She grabbed his lips with hers. He struggled with his pants and her panties for a while and then he was ready for her.

He adjusted her on the bed, spread her legs and slipped inside her, making gentle strokes. She felt a sudden rush of blood in her body. He grabbed her breasts and rolled his tongue over each one of them, while carrying on the gentle movement of his hips. She squealed with ache and joy, and gnawed at his chest with her fingers. Her moans were getting louder and she moved her hips in sync with his.

He brought his mouth closer to hers and kissed her hard on her lips. In the dark too, she could see the man she loved. Suddenly, she switched on the side lamp. Nihal tried to look away. She held his head firmly between her palms and looked deep into his eyes. She looked determined, yet adorable. Their eyes locked and he started building up to bring her to the crest of the biggest wave. Her journey had been beautiful and he wanted the end of the ride to be equally exciting for her. She was screaming with pleasure and her wildness drove him crazy. She bit him hard on the neck as she reached the high point of this beautiful ride and he enjoyed every bit of it as her.

It seemed as if there were just the two of them, cut off from the universe in their own little place. He kissed her forehead. She puckeredher lips and hid her face in his chest. She felt as if she belonged there.

Nihal got up from the bed and entered the washroom. Standing in the shower, he tried to recollect whatever had happened that night in that room. Though he had enjoyed every bit of it, he was not sure if what he did was right. He was not sure how Rabani was going to react to it. He had come here to see her of course and to pep her up. He had heard from Barkat that Rabani was not enjoying the trip at all. He had seen a few candid shots of her sitting alone and staring at phone. She looked pretty but sad in those pictures. So, as soon as he got a chance, he had caught the first flight to Cochin and got into her room with Barkat's help. He had only intended to fool around a bit, but never did he imagine that things would build up and lead to this. What if she blamed him for this? How would he face her then? The more he thought, the more upset he got. He didn't realize for how long he stood in the shower till there was a knock on the door.

"Are you okay?" Rabani asked.

He dried himself and came out. There was food laid on the table and Rabani was instructing the laundry guy to do up Nihal's uniform by morning. She smiled as she saw him coming out and shut the door to the room.

"You must be hungry," she said and signaled him to come for the food.

He saw his favourite chicken biryani laid out.

"Sorry, I ordered without asking you as you were in the shower." She sounded very normal. "Your uniform will be ready by seven. I was not sure what time you would be leaving, but it was really crumpled."

“I don’t have to fly until the day after," he said in a low tone.

“You look tired," she ruffled his hair. “Have a quick bite and get some sleep. You will feel okay by morning.”

Nihal held her hand and made her sit in his lap. “Why are you doing this?”

“Doing what?” She turned towards him.

“You are not upset with whatever happened between us here today?” he asked.

“Why should I be?” She looked surprised. “Or should I be?”

“Believe me, Rabi, I was just trying to fool around a bit. I didn’t know it would lead to this.” Nihal tried to look away.

“So, you regret whatever happened here today?” She turned his face towards her and looked into his eyes.

“Yes. I mean, no. I mean, I don’t know what to say."He was at a loss of words.

“If you are regretting it then it’s really bad for both of us, Nihal.” She stood up. “But I am neither ashamed nor regretful. I love you and I thought you loved me too, and this is a very natural thing to happen between a guy and a girl in love.” She paused. “I am sorry I pulled you into this. Believe me, it was not intentional. One thing just led to another and…”

“Are you serious?” Nihal rose from his chair. “Come here," he held her hand. “Are you blaming yourself for this?”

“Who should I blame then?” Rabani yelped.

"I don't know if I will ever be able to understand you," Nihal shook his head in disbelief and hugged her. "I was thinking that perhaps you would be upset about it. I didn't even ask you."

"You tried to hold back, Nihal; not once, but twice. We both know that. But I didn't want you to stop," she sounded determined.

"I didn't even have a condom," Nihal cut her short.

"Oh my god!" Rabani started laughing. "You are a total Bollywood buff" She continued laughing. "I am going to have my periods in two-three days, so I am in my safe days. I have never had sex before, neither a blood transfusion in my life, so there are no chance of an STD or AIDS. Do you have anything else to say?"

Nihal looked at her like a fool.

"And suppose something happens and people come to know, you just tell them that I forced myself on you. Rather, you should say that I raped you," she winked. "Now don't weigh yourself down with it and have your food." She pulled him to his chair and stuffed a bite in his mouth.

"You will drive me nuts some day, you know," he pulled her hair closer and made her sit next to him.

"Next time, please carry protection whenever you have any plans to fool around with me," she chuckled.

They had their food and hit the bed. "You are amazing, Rabani," he kissed her forehead.

"I know," she smiled.

"Too good for a first timer," he ridiculed her.

"I know," she said.

Chapter 26

Nihal woke up the next morning and found Rabani still there in bed, clinging to him like a child. He turned on his side and rested his head on his hand so that he could see her face. She looked angelic. She was indeed one, he thought.

"One crazy woman you are, you know?" He gently brushed a strand of hair away from her face. "I really don't know what to do with you. But one thing is for sure, it's impossible to stay away from you now." Rabani was still sleeping.

Nihal slid out of the bed and picked up his phone. It was full of New Year's messages and one of them was from Prof. Nirmal too.

'I should call papa,' he thought. 'He didn't respond to my call yesterday. May be I should tell him about Rabani and ask him to speak to Rabani's dad.' He smiled looking at Rabani.

Nihal got ready and slipped out of the room to make a call, so that he didn't disturb Rabani while she was sleeping. He dialed his father's number, but the call was not answered. He tried several times, but he didn't respond. Nihal got worried, so he called up his uncle, his father's elder brother.

"*Sat Sri Akal,* Tayaji," he said as his uncle took the call. "Papa has not been answering my calls since yesterday. I was getting a bit worried."

"He must be at the hospital, I think," his uncle replied. "Neena has not been keeping too well for the past two days. She had those fits again and fell unconscious, so we had to rush her to the hospital," he sighed. "You don't worry, though. She is better now and will hopefully be back home by tomorrow morning. We are all here anyway."

"But papa didn't tell me anything."

"He didn't want you to worry, *beta,*" he replied. "It's not that we all have forgotten Niharika, but your mother's grief is bigger than any of ours. She has lost a child. May *Waheguru* give her the strength to bear it! I am sure she will be alright soon, it's just a matter of time," he paused. "You don't worry and take care of yourself. I will ask Nirmal to speak to you, whenever he gets free," and he disconnected.

Nihal sat down on a bench and started to think about the things at home, his father, his mother and the gloominess that had engulfed the peace and happiness of their lives. Such thoughts swallowed up his enthusiasm to speak to his father about Rabani too.

'I have no right to pull her into this. What kind of a life could she have with me in that house? How is Ma going to react to seeing her around? How will Rabi cope up with all this?' The thoughts pulled him down and his eyes were flooded.

Rabani woke up and looked around for Nihal, but he was not there in the room. 'He must have gone for a jog,' she thought and dressed up quickly. Looking at her image in the mirror, she felt beautiful and blushed thinking about the night before. She went around the hotel to look for him, but she couldn't find him anywhere.

Then, she found him sitting on a bench in a farther corner of the hotel backyard.

"You scared me, Nihal," she said as she approached him.

Nihal tried to wipe the tears away from his face quickly, but it didn't go unnoticed.

"What happened? Why are you sitting here?" she stood next to him.

Nihal shook his head.

"Nihal, are you okay? Is all well at home? Your mom, dad..."

Nihal clang to her before she could finish and started snuffling.

Rabani got anxious and held him tightly, trying to comfort him. "Please tell me what is bothering you, Nihal. I think I have the right to know."

"Ma is in the hospital."

"Why? I mean what happened to her?" Rabani asked. "You said she didn't keep too well. What is the problem with her?"

Nihal made her sit next to him. "Rabi, it was never like this with her or with all of us. We were very happy in our little world; Ma, papa, I and Niharika, my twin."

"I know you have a sister, I saw her picture at your place."

"She is no longer with us. We lost her two years ago to an accident," Nihal said slowly.

Rabani was stunned to hear that.

"She was beautiful just like Ma and intelligent like papa. She was the apple of everyone's eye. She used to fight with me all the time that Ma and Papa loved her more than they loved me. We used to sing together; Ma, Niharika and I." Nihal held her hand, "Two and a half years ago, we got her married to the boy she loved. We were all very happy, but that happiness didn't last for too long." He paused.

"A week after her wedding, she was coming to visit us with her husband. I still remember, my mother cooked all her favorite dishes for dinner. Actually, I was supposed to go and get her from her in-laws' place but my brother-in-law, Amrit, called up and said that he would bring her with him. We were waiting for them eagerly but instead of her, we got a phone call that she had met with an accident. Amrit had called us up. We couldn't believe it and rushed to the hospital where she had been taken." Nihal sighed as if trying to catch some air. Tears rolled down his cheeks.

After a minute, he continued, "Amrit and Niharika were coming home in their car. The door on her side was not properly locked and they didn't realize it. She was not even wearing the seat belt, apparently. At a sharp turn, the door got unlocked, she fell out from the car and was crushed by a truck following right behind their car. She died on the spot. Amrit had been with her, but couldn't do anything. When we reached the hospital, she was declared dead on arrival. We all were devastated. The doctors didn't want us to see her body as her head was badly crushed, but Ma insisted on seeing her regardless. The moment the sheet was removed, we had in front of us a sight beyond anyone's imagination." Nihal was sobbing loudly now.

Rabani patted his back gently and tried to comfort him.

"My mother lost her senses and has not been the same since then. That day, I not only lost my sister but my Ma too." Nihal's voice was choked.

Rabani was shocked on hearing this story. She held him in her arms and tried to appease him.

When he was a little better, he continued, "Since then, my mother has not been very stable mentally. She is sick all the time. Papa left his job to be with her. She doesn't go anywhere. At times, she slips back into depression. She starts making phone calls to my sister, asking her when she would come home. She starts cooking food for her. Sometimes, she throws away a ready meal from the dining table. Her reactions are very unpredictable. We avoid visitors because she becomes violent at times. Papa is trying to deal with the situation. I don't know if I will ever get my Ma back," he said and started crying again.

Rabani kept holding him in her arms.

"I saw my sister's body too. For two years after that, even I could not sleep peacefully. I used to have nightmares of her accident and see her taking my Ma and papa away with her. She used to tease me even in my dreams that Ma loves her more than me and seeing Ma's condition, I think she was right," he was snivelling again. "Niharika and I used to sing together, but after she was gone, I could never sing again. I lost my peace of mind, my singing and my parents too. To some extent, I feel I am responsible for her death too. I wish I had gone that day to get her."

"Don't say that, Nihal," Rabani looked into his eyes. "You didn't know this could happen."

"When my father saw me in that state, he asked Neil to take me away to Bangalore so that I could start afresh at least. But that didn't help either. I shifted to Bangalore, but my life seemed to have gotten stuck at that one moment. My father tried to comfort me and Ma both as much as he could. Neil tried his best to pull me out of this as well," Nihal sighed.

"I can't imagine what you have been going through, Nihal," Rabani was herself choked with emotion. "I had always thought of you as a happy-go-lucky guy, but you have been carrying so much in your heart and I couldn't do anything for you."

"No, you are wrong, Rabani. You are the one who pulled me out of it bit by bit, though you knew nothing about it." He smiled weakly at her. "One day, I saw you in Bangalore," he started again. "I saw you and in no time, you vanished." He held her hand. "That night in my dream, I saw you standing with me when Niharika snatched Ma's hand from mine. For the first time in two years, I slept so peacefully that Neil got scared thinking that I was dead. I went to the same place searching for you many times after, but couldn't find you. That day, I had seen you talking to a guard, and I went after his life to find out about you. After trying for weeks, he told me your name and that you don't live in Bangalore anymore. I was back to square one. Then one day, I saw you at the airport started following you. You know the rest of it. I got my singing back and my peace of mind too. I had you to think about all the time, so no other thought ever bothered me after that. I started to visit my parents more often, just to be with you in Delhi and it made a difference in my father's life at least. It feels as if you will never leave my hand," Nihal hugged Rabani. "You don't know what you have done for me."

He continued, "You've met papa, and he too liked you. Believe you me, Rabi, I loved that you went to see my parents, but I was just scared for you. I didn't know how ma would react on seeing you there. You cooked for papa. He was touched, as no one had done this for him in a long time. You know, he calls you *bitiya.* That is how he used to address Niharika," Nihal smiled. "I know he wants to meet you again, but I don't want to drag you into all this."

"Everything will be fine, Nihal. It's just a matter of time. I am sure that just like you, your parents too will come out of this someday. You just need to wait for the right time." She gently patted his back. "If He takes away something from us, He blesses us in many other ways. All you need to do is just to believe in Him. I am sure He has a plan for you and your Ma too." Rabani held Nihal close to her.

"Nihal, I did meet your dad at Mannat's reception," Rabani said slowly. Nihal looked up at her in surprise.

"Yes. I don't know what you told him about me, but he asked me to be by your side always," she paused and looked into his eyes. "And believe me, I will never leave your hand as long as it comforts you."

"But why did you not tell me this before?"

"I didn't want to annoy you. You had asked me to wait till you tell me everything anyway. I had tried to avoid him but he found me." She shrugged and looked at Nihal. "Your father loves you a lot and is worried about you all the time. I think he needs you. Try to be with your parents as much as you can. You know your mom is suffering, but you don't realize what you dad is going through. He too lost his daughter to that accident, and to some extent his wife and son too," she said sadly. "Even he needs your care and attention. I don't know if he is taking care of his health or not, if he is seeing his doctor regularly or not."

"What is with his health? He is absolutely fine," Nihal interrupted.

"Your dad is a BP patient and is on regular medication," Rabani said in a low tone.

Nihal looked at her in surprise. "How do you know that? I have never seen him take any medicine."

"I don't want you to blame yourself for this, but I saw him having his medicine, the same that my mum takes for high BP. He doesn't go out of the house because of your mom, but he himself is so stressed besides that because of this accident and your mom's illness. Nihal, you can't shut your eyes and think that all is well at home. It's high time you take charge of things and do the needful for your parents. The past has to be left behind. Whatever you have in hand now, you'll have to make a difference with that only," Rabani said firmly.

Nihal nodded and hid his face in Rabani's lap. "Hmmm, you are right."

"If possible, take off from work for a while and be with them. Let me know if I can do anything as well. One more thing," she paused. "You will always share with me whatever there is and however bad it is. Every problem has a solution and we can work it out together," Rabani said and kissed his hair.

"Now, let's go and have breakfast. I am starving; someone sucked away all my energy last night," she chuckled when she found that Nihal felt a little better too.

"What else did papa say?" Nihal asked.

"Your papa said that his son is an idiot and that I should pull his ears," she laughed and pulled at his hand to make him stand on his feet.

The New Year brought with it a new beginning in Nihal's life - a year full of hope, love, laughter and new dreams.

Chapter 27

Tejas was insisting that his parents should come and stay with him. But with Resham's responsibility on them, they were not able to take a decision. Rabani came to their rescue then. She suggested that after Resham finishes her 12th class, she would get Resham enrolled in a college in Bangalore, as Rabani's office was shifting her back to Bangalore too. Barkat, Resham and she could all stay together. Since Mannat and Neil were in Bangalore too, Col. Sandhu agreed for it. It was decided that in April, after Resham's exams got over, they would shift her to Bangalore.

Meanwhile, Rabani and Nihal were busy in their own world. They exploited every possible opportunity to be with each other. Nihal loved the way Rabani cooked for him and fed him irrespective of her busy office schedule. He enjoyed all the love, care and attention he was getting. This was one thing that had been lacking in his life for all those years, so he was thrilled. He missed no chance to be with her. Life seemed to be sorted for him, but was it really?

It was February; still a month and a half before Rabani was to move to Bangalore. She had a meeting in Bangalore the next day, so she thought of reaching there an evening before.

'I will get more time with Nihal,' she thought while boarding the flight.

When she reached Nihal's place, she found him lying in bed. He was complaining of acute pain in his stomach and was already looking pale and weak. Rabani was scared to the core. She immediately called up Barkat and explained the situation to her. Barkat asked her to get Nihal to a hospital as early as possible.

"I am suspecting appendicitis," said Barkat.

Rabani called for a cab and rushed Nihal to the hospital. Barkat was already waiting there for them. The diagnosis was done and the doctors decided to operate on Nihal as his appendix had gotten inflamed badly. Rabani tried to contact Neil, but he was not reachable.

She thought of informing Prof. Nirmal but Nihal stopped her, "No, he would worry. Leaving Ma alone is not possible anyway, so don't inform him. You are here with me, I will be fine," he said and Rabani agreed.

The surgery was done and Nihal was shifted to a private room late at night. Neil and Mannat reached there by then too. "Thank you, Rabi," Neil said.

Mannat was trying to understand the situation, not aware still that Nihal and Rabani were seeing each other. "What were you doing here? What's cooking, guys?" she looked at Neil and Rabani.

"I love your sister, Mannat, and she loves me too," Nihal replied.

"You can't be sane, Rabi," Mannat was agitated. "If I am not wrong, you know about it too," she looked at Neil.

Neil tried to calm her down.

"You all are crazy. How is this possible? Nihal is not your type at all, Rabi. You will never be happy with him, I know," Mannat said harshly.

Rabani interrupted, "I am happy, Mannat. Besides, he is no longer the guy you knew back in college. He has grown up. In fact, we all have." She held Mannat's hand, "When you chose to be with Neil, we all respected your decision. So now, even if you think it silly, I expect you to respect my decision too."

Mannat shook her head in dismay and said, "I sincerely pray that I am proved wrong about Nihal. I am worried because I don't want you to get hurt." She hugged Rabani. "And you, Nihal, dare you do any nonsense with her, I won't leave you," she warned Nihal with teary eyes.

Nihal tried to get up and signaled Mannat to come near him. Mannat went to sit next to him. He held her hand and said, "I wish I could make you understand what she means to me." He looked at Rabani. "Hurting her is the last thing I can think of doing in my life. She means everything to me, like Neil does to you. The only difference is that you two are married, while I and Rabani are not, but that is not reason enough to doubt my sincerity. Take me for my word, I will always be with her."

Mannat patted his hand and smiled, "Don't get me wrong, but I was worried for my little sister."

"Don't worry, Nihal loves her a lot. I have seen it myself, Mannat," said Neil.

For the next few days, Rabani stayed with Nihal. When Nihal got a little better, he informed Prof. Nirmal about the surgery.

"Who is there with you? I am coming tomorrow," he said.

"No, papa. I am fine now. Neil and Mannat are here and Mannat's cousin Barkat is my doctor, so you needn't worry. Moreover, Ma is there. She can't be left alone. I will visit you as soon as I am discharged from the hospital." He didn't mention anything about Rabani.

Prof. Nirmal had expected Rabani to be there with him, but was disappointed when he didn't hear any mention of her. 'I have been thinking too much, maybe there is nothing between them.'

The day Nihal was getting discharged, he gave his credit card to clear the bills, but none of his cards worked. Rabani quietly cleared the bills. Later when she checked for him, she found that his credit card bills were long overdue.

"An action can be taken against you anytime for recovery. Don't you understand that?" she squeaked.

I don't know, I always forget to pay them. My account hardly has any money. I don't know where my money goes. My salary comes to the bank, I get alerts on my phone, but it never reflects in my account. But whenever I go to withdraw money from the ATM, I get as much as I want, so I never bothered," he shrugged.

Looking at his face, Rabani started laughing. "And you never tried to find out? You are coming to the bank with me tomorrow. Let's sort this out first."

At the bank, Rabani got Nihal's account checked. In his salary account, he had lakhs of rupees, but all of it was going into auto-FDRs. That is why they never reflected in his account balance. He had some old FDRs done from his account and had a few tax saving plans too. Money was getting auto-debited from his account for their payments, and he was not even aware of it. Rabani laughed at Nihal's financial expertise.

"Niharika used to look after all that. I never bothered to look at this side. As far as finance management goes, I know nothing."

"Your sister has done a good job for you, let's do a few more things."

She got his credit card bills cleared, bought him a family health insurance plan, set reminders for credit card and premium payments, gave auto-debit instructions, wherever possible, and checked out some investment plans for him too. In no time, she had sorted out half his problems.

"We need to file your income tax return too."

"We will do that, but after lunch," Nihal suggested. "If you will solve all my problems, how will I live without them? Let's leave some of them for some other time. You are going back in the evening today and I will be all alone then. How will I manage with neither you nor my problems around?"

"I have a better idea. You sit down and think of how you are going to spend this money," she replied. "You can even buy a bungalow right away, Mr. Bajwa."

"Good idea, Rabi. Let's buy a house. You are shifting to Bangalore soon, we will live together in our own house," he sounded excited.

Rabani started laughing, "You are impossible, Nihal."

Nihal's life seemed to be back on track.

Chapter 28

Rabani shifted to Bangalore and moved in with Barkat. Her old roommate and friend had left. Resham joined both of them after a few days too. Rabani got her enrolled in a degree college. Mannat insisted that Rabani should stay with her, but she turned her down saying that she didn't want to disturb the newly married couple during their honeymoon period. Moreover, Nihal lived in the same building as Barkat, so she thought it better to live there only. Col. Sandhu and his wife moved with their son to England. The hub of activities shifted from Delhi to Bangalore.

Though Rabani had jokingly told him to invest in buying a house, Nihal took it seriously. He started looking for properties in and around Bangalore. "It's a nice city and besides, I met you here. So Bangalore will always have a special place in my life."

They homed in on a spectacular three bedroom villa with a beautiful courtyard, and booked it. The project was still under construction. Rabani negotiated to get the best price for Nihal. The builder agreed to reduce the price if fifty percent of the payment was done within a week, and the rest at various stages during the construction. Nihal had enough funds with him, but he needed ten lakhs more to make the down payment. Rabani agreed to give him the money on a condition that he could return it to her later, while for the remaining amount, Nihal applied for a loan. Later, Nihal tried to return the money to her many times, but she refused, saying that the house belonged to her too, so she wouldn't take the money back.

Nihal, Rabani, Barkat, Mannat, Neil and Resham had a good time in Bangalore. For Nihal and Rabani, as well as Neil and Mannat, that was the best time of their lives. Whenever they had an off day or were free in the evenings, there used to be a house party. Resham was an excellent cook and took charge of the kitchen. Nihal got his guitar from Delhi and they had many musical evenings. Together they took many weekend trips to holiday destinations. At times, Barkat and Resham joined them too.

Whenever Rabani had official trips, Nihal started to accompany her whenever he could. On one such trip, Rabani had to go to England. Her office was sending her for some assignment there.

"How will I manage without you here, that too for two whole weeks?" he argued with Rabani.

"I miss my family, so it's good. I will get to spend some time with them too," she replied.

"No, you belong only to me. I will come along," Nihal hugged her. "And remember that lock, you can't break it open."

Rabani started laughing at this childlike behaviour. "No, you can't come with me. What will my parents think? They know nothing about us, Nihal."

So, it was decided that Rabani would go by herself and Nihal would join her later.

Rabani went to England and got to spend time with her family along with her work too. As decided, Nihal joined her there after one week.

“I am in England to meet my uncle, so I thought of visiting you too," he informed Col. Sandhu. “And of course, not to miss auntie’s yummy food.”

“So, you couldn’t be without her even for a few days?” Samaira teased him when she found Nihal alone.

“I can’t, you see," he replied.

“I think it’s high time we should think about you two and get you married," Samaira pulled his ear.

Nihal was jolted into reality, as he had not been thinking on those lines. He knew that he loved Rabani and she loved him too, but marriage was something he was scared of. So he just smiled and kept quiet.

On their way back, Nihal thought of bringing this up with Rabani. “What do you think of marriage?”

“Marriage is a beautiful institution, a bond shared by two people. However different they may be from each other, they accept each other with all their differences and shortcomings,” she explained.

“So, you believe in marriage?” He asked.

“Yes," she nodded. “And you?”

“I believe in love, Rabani. Marriage is more like a social obligation to me," he tried to discourage her.

Rabani was stunned because back home, her mom had been asking her to think about getting married and had even hinted that everyone at home liked Nihal. She had been planning to speak to his family once she was back in India.

"Why do you think it's an obligation?" she asked weakly.

"Look around, how many people do you see happy after marriage? Look at my parents, what kind of a life are they living?"

"You are wrong here, Nihal. If you consider your parents' case, then you should blame it on love. Your dad is suffering because he loves your mom and doesn't want to leave her alone in her pain. He wants to be with her all the time. And your mom is suffering because of love too, her love for her daughter."

Nihal fell quiet after that, but Rabani was not at peace. 'He loves me, but he is not okay with the idea of marriage. And there, my mom is planning something else. How am I going to deal with all that once she is back in India? Are we going to live like this all our lives? I too love Nihal, so much that I can't imagine a life without him.' The more she thought, the more stressed she was. She decided not to bring this up with Nihal again. 'If he is not ready for a commitment, I will never force him. This is something that should come from within, it can't be forced upon.'

Time was flying. Barkat had applied for a job at a hospital in Delhi and was hopeful to get that. Col. and Mrs. Sandhu were back from their UK trip. Rabani and Resham got Resham's son to Bangalore and got him admitted in a school there, since Resham used to miss him all the time. Mannat and Neil were expecting their first child and the entire family was excited to welcome the new member into the family. Rabani's mom had thus shelved the issue of her marriage for the time being.

At Nihal's house too, there was some improvement in his mother's condition. She was seeing a new doctor, Dr. Sartaj, whose treatment really worked for her. Prof. Nirmal had started taking Neena out for walk regularly. Nihal joined them at times too, whenever he was in Delhi. They had joined a yoga class as well. Neena didn't have those fits so frequently anymore. She had become active on social media again. Prof, Nirmal thought it to be good for her too, as she was finally doing something besides thinking about their daughter.

Nihal and Rabani were busy in their own little world that they had created for themselves, where there were no shadows of Nihal's past and no pressure from Rabani's family to get married. Rabani was all about giving whatever she could, never expecting anything in return. "All I need is love and respect from you. I can live without everything else till the time I see love in your heart and respect in your eyes for me," she told Nihal on one such occasion when he asked what he should get her for her birthday.

Chapter 29

Barkat joined her new job in Delhi and was very happy with it. Her mother too was happy to have her around again. Both her sons were already married and now she wanted Barkat to settle down in life too, so that she could be free from her responsibilities which she had been managing all alone since her husband's death. Col. Sandhu and his wife had stood by her all the time and she was grateful to them for it.

It didn't take too long for the wedding bells to ring for Barkat. Dr. Sartaj Grewal was the son of a doctor duo. He was a psychiatrist and worked at the same hospital as Barkat. His father, Dr. Grewal, was a heart-specialist and his mother, a gynaecologist. Barkat and Sartaj got to know each other at work and he mentioned her to his parents. The families met, and Barkat and Sartaj got engaged at a simple ceremony in the presence of their elders.

Rabani was very happy for her cousin, but somewhere deep down she also felt worried that her own mother would now bring up the issue of her marriage too. Barkat suggested this to Rabani too that she and Nihal should start thinking about taking their relationship to next level. Rabani had nothing to say to her. What could she have said, that Nihal didn't want to get married?

One day, Nihal was at Neil's place. Mannat had moved to her parents' as her delivery date was approaching. Neil and Nihal were having breakfast.

Raman handed over a Parantha to Nihal and said, "Neil is going to be a dad soon. What are your plans regarding getting married?"

"My plans?" Nihal retorted. "Auntie, if everyone will get married and be with his wife, who will look after you?"

"My daughter- in-laws," she replied.

"Yes, Nihal. Even I wanted to ask you this. Mannat's parents were asking me to speak to you that if you are interested, they could speak to your dad for you and Rabani," Neil said.

Raman was excited. "Yes, Rabani is a wonderful girl. You can't find anyone better than her. I have known her since she was a little girl. Take my word for it, there can't be a better girl for you than Rabani."

Ahana backed her as well, "She is so beautiful and I like her too, Veerji."

"But she is not as pretty as auntie," Nihal tried to divert from the topic.

Raman rolled her eyes at Nihal and left for the kitchen.

"I am serious, Nihal," Neil said sternly. "Her parents are worried. I think they have an idea that you are seeing Rabani. Moreover, there is lot of pressure on Rabani too. You should talk to your father."

Nihal thought for a while and said, "I don't know, it's all going fine between me and her. We both love each other, but I have never thought of marriage. She never mentioned anything about it either. Moreover, I am not ready for all this."

Neil was shocked. "What do you mean, Nihal? You love her but you don't want to marry her? And you want it to go on this way? Are you nuts? What do you mean she's never said anything? Did you ever ask her?"

"Neil, I don't want to get married, though I will be with her all my life. I can't leave her ever, but the thought of marriage scares me. It sounds weird to me," Nihal said firmly.

On hearing this, Neil left the food on his plate and got up from his chair. After thinking for a while, he replied harshly, "If you have no plans to marry her, it's better you stay away from her. She is like my sister and I don't appreciate the presence of a man like you around her, who is hell bent on spoiling her life. Do you have any idea how much pressure she is under from her family, and how she is dealing with it? You say you don't even know what she wants. After so many months of being with her, if you don't even know this then she is with the wrong guy."

Nihal had not expected this. He got up too and left without saying a word to Neil.

Mrs. Sandhu brought up this topic with Rabani a couple of times as well, insisting that she should think seriously about getting married. "You are going to be twenty seven soon and it's high time you should start thinking about getting married."

"Mom, I am just 27. Mannat got married at 28, so there's a year left for me still. Moreover, I am expecting a promotion at work soon, so I don't want to think about marriage till then," she said, turning down Mrs. Sandhu's suggestion.

However, she didn't budge. "Mannat had decided much before she turned 28 who she was going to marry, and as far as promotion goes, who says that married girls can't get a promotion?"

Mannat backed her mother too. "Yes Rabi, I think you should start thinking about this seriously. If you want, we could speak to Nihal."

"No one is going to ask anything from anyone. I will let you all know whenever I am ready to marry," Rabani asserted. Though she had conveyed her point to everyone, Mrs. Sandhu was still not convinced.

Mannat brought this up with Neil that he should speak to Nihal about this. Though Neil assured Mannat that he would, he was not sure what to ask Nihal who had already made his point clear to him that he didn't want to marry. Neil thought of speaking to Rabani about this.

"You and Nihal should think about taking your relationship to the next step, "Neil casually suggested to Rabani one fine day.

"He is your friend and I am sure you know what his views are about marriage," she replied.

"And what do you want, Rabi?"

"I don't know, Neil. I have stopped thinking about it. All I know is that I am happy being with him and I don't want to force him for something that he is not comfortable with."

"And what about your family? How long will you be able to avoid this topic at home?" Neil asked with concern.

"I don't know, Neil. I have no idea. I can't beg Nihal to marry me, so it doesn't matter what I want. All I can do is avoid visiting my parents for a while and then hopefully, they will leave for England in a few months again and things will get easier for me, for sometime at least." Rabani sounded very helpless.

Neil didn't know what to tell her. 'You are an idiot, Nihal. You have no idea what you are doing to her,' Neil thought.

Nihal was really disturbed with what Neil had asked him to do back at his house. Staying away from Rabani was impossible for him. He tried his best to avoid her, but this was beyond his control. Many a times he thought of not meeting her again, but the resolution could only last for a few hours and then, by the end of the day, he would find himself at Rabani's house again on the pretext of something or the other.

The day he wouldn't go to meet her, she would land up at his place and storm him with a barrage of questions, "Where were you? Are you alright?" and he would fall for her again.

Nihal did not meet Neil for a long time after their argument. 'How long can we continue avoiding each other?' Nihal thought and went to meet Neil one day. "Are you still upset with me?" he asked Neil.

"No," Neil shook his head.

"I tried to stay away from her, Neil, but I can't. Whenever I get an off from work, I go home, but nothing seems to help. I can't keep her off my mind or my life."

"You know what you should do, Nihal. I don't understand, what is the problem in getting married when you know you can't live without her?"

"You know the situation at home. My mom gets paranoid over just about anything. I don't know if she will ever come to accept a new member in the house. I don't want to drag Rabani into all this either. She comes from a close knit family, while at my place, all she is going to have is stress, worry, problems and sorrow. Do you think it's fair to ruin her life like that? Will just my love be enough for her to be happy? She deserves much more in life, Neil. I won't be able to give her anything."

Hearing this, Neil was relieved to some extent. "You are thinking too much, Nihal. This is not as serious as you think." Though he kept quiet in front of Nihal, he decided to bring this up with Prof. Nirmal whenever he would meet him next.

Chapter 30

Mannat and Neil were blessed with a baby boy whom they named Sooraj. Everyone at home was thrilled. Little Sooraj filled their lives with joy and happiness. Sandhu's had one more reason to be happy. Sartaj and Barkat's wedding was fixed for 5th January. Though there were more than two months left for the wedding, the preparations had begun already.

Though Rabani was not visiting Delhi much those days so as to avoid the uncalled for discussion on her marriage, but when she heard of little Sooraj, she couldn't stop herself. Rabani had a meeting in the city too, so she came to Delhi. She was excited that she would get to spend some time with her nephew.

Nihal was not visiting Rabani's parents a lot anymore too. From the time he heard that Rabani's mother might bring his and Rabani's wedding issue up, he avoided visiting them. Nihal had to go to Hong Kong for some training session for three weeks, so he thought that he should go and meet Mannat and Sooraj before leaving for Hong Kong.

Neil went to Nihal's house to inform Prof. Nirmal about Sooraj's birth. He wanted to speak to him about Nihal and Rabani, as he was sure that Prof. Nirmal would have a better solution for this problem. When Prof. Nirmal heard about Sooraj, he was very happy and congratulated Neil, "It feels so good to hear that I am a granduncle now." He enquired about the well being of Col. Sandhu and his family, to which Neil said that they were fine.

"How is Rabani?" Prof. Nirmal asked suddenly.

"She is good too, uncle." Neil was surprised as he didn't know that Prof. Nirmal knew about her.

"She had come to invite us for your wedding. Sweet girl! But I never saw her again after your wedding."

"That is because she doesn't live in Delhi," Neil replied.

Neil thought it to be a good time to discuss about Nihal and Rabani. "Uncle, we should start thinking about getting Nihal married. It's high time now."

Before Prof. Nirmal could say anything, Neena joined them and hugged Neil. "How are you? And where are you these days? I am seeing you after months."

"Stop scolding him, he is a dad now," Prof. Nirmal said.

Her reaction was not what Neil had expected. She was excited. "How are Mannat and the baby? Professor, we will go to meet them one of these days."

Neil didn't want to upset her so he didn't talk about the matter of Nihal's wedding any further.

"We surely will, Neena." He looked at Neil, "Neil is saying that we should start thinking of getting Nihal married now. What you think, Neena?"

"Yes, I feel the same, Professor. I will speak to him when he is in Delhi next. We have already delayed it long enough."

'At last, it's happening,' Neil thought as he left Nihal's house.

Nihal landed in Delhi and took a cab straight for Rabani's house. "Where is my nephew?" he shouted as he entered Rabani's house.

"First, you meet his grandfather. Where have you been all these days?" Col. Sandhu complained.

Nihal hugged him, "Sorry, uncle. I was a little busy with work."

He entered Mannat's room, and found Rabani sitting there too. He met with Mannat and Sooraj and lifted him in his arms. "You are soooo tiny," he started playing with the baby.

Little Sooraj mewled, so he handed him back to Mannat. "He has taken after his mom and doesn't like uncle Nihal much." He spoke to Maninder for a minute and then went out of the room to sit with Col. Sandhu.

"Nihal is here, I should tell him that we want to meet his parents," Mrs. Sandhu sounded excited.

"Mom, what is this? He has come to meet Mannat and Sooraj," Rabani replied.

"I know, but what is the harm if I talk to him about this?"

"Yes mom, you should ask to meet his parents," Mannat backed her mother.

"Are you all crazy? Am I a burden here that you guys want to get rid of? Do I have a say in my wedding matter or not? The way you talk, mom, it seem as if I am a problem for all of you that you want to put away on someone else as soon as possible. What would he think that he came here to meet Sooraj, and you people want to trap him for your daughter? It's so embarrassing. This is the reason I don't come home." Rabani's eyes welled up.

As Nihal came to sit with Col. Sandhu, he realized that he had left his phone back in Mannat's room. As he went back towards the room, he heard the entire conversation between Rabani and her mother and sister. He also heard her sobbing.

'Neil was right; she is going through so much.' He came back to sit with Col. Sandhu.

Col. Sandhu asked for coffee, so Rabani came out of the room and went to the kitchen. As she was making coffee, Nihal came to the kitchen too.

"I didn't expect to meet you here today," she tried to smile with teary eyes.

Nihal held her and hugged her tightly. "I love you, Rabani." Tears rolled down his cheeks.

"What happened, Nihal?" She got worried. "Are you alright? Why are you crying? Is your mom alright?"

"Nothing," he shook his head. "You know, you don't need to be so good. You should have told me about this." He released Rabani, picked up his mobile from Mannat's room and left saying that he had some work. Rabani couldn't understand anything.

Nihal couldn't stay there. Though he had already heard this from Neil, he actually realized that day what Rabani had been facing at home.' That is why she doesn't come to Delhi these days. She didn't even mention it to me. Even today, she was posing a smile so that I don't come to know,'

Nihal kept thinking on his way to home. 'Why the hell do you love me so much? I don't know if I even deserve you.'

Nihal reached home and found that there were some guests visiting at his place. Her mother's old friend Meera was there with her husband and her daughter, Kritika. They had shifted to Canada a few years back. Unwillingly, Nihal went to sit with them. Nihal's mother was very happy to see her friend.

"We are thinking of getting Nihal married," she told her friend.

Prof. Nirmal smiled seeing that his wife was taking the thought of Nihal's marriage positively.

Neena looked at Nihal and said, "I am looking for a girl for you. Your Papa and I think that you should settle down now."

"Whatever you feel is right, mom," Nihal said uninterestedly, as he was already drained out physically and mentally. After sometime, he excused himself saying that he was unwell and wanted to take some rest.

"Papa, I will be going to Hong Kong for three weeks, so I will see you after a month now," Nihal informed his father later that evening.

"Okay. Meanwhile, I will look for some suitable matches for you," Neena replied. Nihal smiled at his mother. She was looking better that day.

Chapter 31

It was a usual Monday morning. Nihal reported at the airport and checked his schedule. 'Hopefully, I will be back early today. It's Rabani's birthday tomorrow and I should be here to bring in her birthday.' Nihal wanted to spend some time with her before leaving for Hong Kong. He was sure that she wouldn't go home, especially after knowing what all she was facing at home. His mind was flooded with the memories of her birthday two years ago, when he had confessed to her that he loved her. She never parted with the pendant that he had given her. Even at Mannat's wedding, she was wearing it along with the other necklace. The thought brought a smile to his face. "I love you, Ms. Sandhu," he murmured.

Till the afternoon, the day seemed like any other day. He had many take-offs and landings. On his way back from Kochi to Bangalore, he was informed a little short of entering the city that they wouldn't be able to land at the Bangalore airport as a plane had skidded on the runway. The ground operation was on and the runway was temporarily closed. Nihal was thus asked to divert to Mangalore.

"I might be late, but I will still try to make it for her birthday somehow." He pushed away his thoughts and got busy with the flight proceedings.

The plane was approaching Mangalore and he was preparing to land there when he realized that the landing gear was not getting engaged. The display panel showed three red lights. He informed the ATC at Mangalore about it. After a bit of contemplation, he was asked to divert to Goa, but since they had already been diverted from Bangalore, the aircraft didn't have sufficient fuel to be diverted any further. In the serious business of aviation, every take-off is optional but every landing is mandatory, so he had no choice but to land there.

Mangalore had a table-top runway with the air strip length shorter than usual. Usually too, pilots were extra careful while landing in Mangalore. In this case however, when a longer runway length was of the utmost requirement, it was very risky to land with a faulty gear.

He cautioned the cabin crew and all the necessary arrangements were made within and outside the plane. On the plane's P.A. system, Nihal explained the situation to the passengers and requested them to cooperate.

He tried to keep his cool, but under these circumstances it was very difficult to do so. He closed his eyes for a minute and thought of his parents, 'Are they going to lose their other child too?' His parents' sad faces made him go weak and he opened his eyes.

It was time to deal with the situation. He attempted the landing as he was guided. He reduced the speed just enough to maintain the direction and switched off all the electric equipments just before landing. The plane landed on its belly, as expected, with a loud thud, followed by an extended screeching sound.

Nihal had done his bit and everything was now in His hands. The plane kept moving. No one was sure of what would happen, not even Nihal. Everyone inside and outside the plane watched with bated breaths as the plane rolled forward.

Nihal closed his eyes and thought of Rabani. "I really love you, Rabi. I wish to be able to see you again." He started to have nostalgic flashes of the time spent with her. "Please God, I want to see her again. I want to be with her," he said a silent prayer.

The plane slowed down and stopped at the end of the runway, turning to one side. The airport crew was ready for all kinds of emergencies, and handled the situation outside the plane well. Nihal announced the safe landing through the P.A. system. The passengers started cheering and clapping.

Nihal's hands were cold as ice. He held his head in his hands and whispered, "I am coming to you, Rabi."

His co-pilot got up from his seat and hugged him. "We have landed safely," he whispered weakly.

All the passengers and cabin crew disembarked. With the grace of God, no one had suffered any major injuries. By that evening, the news was in the media too.

'Papa must be worried,' Nihal thought and dialled Prof. Nirmal's number as soon as he got free and told him all about the incident and that he was safe.

His father had already got the news from the television, but he didn't know that his son was flying that plane. Prof. Nirmal thanked God for being kind this time.

There were no flights for Bangalore that day, so Nihal had no choice but to stay in Mangalore that night. He was too tired to go by road, so he checked in to a hotel. He tried calling Rabani, but she didn't take the call. So, Nihal left a message, "I am stuck somewhere, will see you tomorrow. I have got to tell you something, Rabi. Call me whenever you are free."

Neil too came to hear about this and called Nihal.

"I am fine, Neil. You needn't worry. I will see you tomorrow. You were right, I should sort things out with Rabi. I can't keep her hanging. I have made up my mind. You too will get to know tomorrow. My battery is dying, so I will speak to you later."

The day had been very eventful otherwise as well. Resham's son Bunny had come back from school that day with a high fever. Resham got him to a hospital and the doctor informed her that Bunny needed to be kept under observation. When Nihal called, Rabani had been speaking to the doctor about Bunny, so she couldn't take the call.

Resham asked Rabani to go home, but she insisted on staying back in the hospital. "Di, you have been on your toes all day. You need to catch up on your sleep. Meanwhile, I will sit with Bunny."

She saw Nihal's message and tried to call him, but his phone was switched off. His phone's battery had given up.

In Delhi, Mannat was enjoying her new-found motherhood to the fullest. She wanted to capture every minute of Sooraj's day, so she clicked a lot of pictures of little Sooraj and posted them to friends and family. That day too, she had clicked some pictures of Sooraj and was uploading them on Facebook. She was going through the various posts on her feed when a certain post shocked her.

"Wedding bells for Nihal," she read.

The post was from Nihal's mom and he was tagged in it. His parents were announcing his upcoming engagement to some girl called Kritika. Mannat was stunned. She took a screen shot of the post and forwarded the message to Neil and Rabani.

Neil checked the message. He was shocked too. *You too will come to know about it tomorrow,* Nihal's words echoed in his head. 'Is this what he wants to tell me? How can you even think of doing this, Nihal?' Neil was furious. He tried Nihal's number, but his phone was switched off. So, Neil called Mannat back and asked her not to tell Rabani about it till he reached her. Mannat couldn't dare to tell Neil that she had already messaged her.

Mannat immediately called Rabani up. "How are you?" she asked.

"I am fine," Rabani replied.

"Did you see the picture?" Mannat asked hurriedly.

"Yea, I did," she lied. Rabani thought that Mannat had sent her some picture of Sooraj.

"How could he do this?" Mannat said.

"It's okay, Mannat. Don't be mad at him," Rabani replied. She thought it was some cute naughtiness of Sooraj that she had shared with her, since Mannat kept sending her his pictures all the time those days, showing her how naughty Sooraj was growing up to be, so she said," I was sure he would do something like that."

Mannat couldn't understand. "Are you okay, Rabani?"

"Yeah, I am fine. It's just that office is very hectic these days. I am tired, so will probably sleep now," Rabani said and disconnected the call. Mannat was puzzled at her reaction.

Neena was very excited those days. She wanted Nihal to get married as soon as possible. She had even spoken to her friend Meera if she liked Nihal for her daughter. Meera too assured her that once Nihal would return from Hong Kong, they would discuss it with him. Neena, in her excitement however, posted it on Facebook. Later that night when Prof. Nirmal saw the post, he deleted it, but the harm had already been done.

Nihal looked at his watch. It was 12 o'clock. His phone's battery had died so he asked the operator to connect to Rabani. The network had congestion though, so the line didn't get through.

"Happy Birthday, Rabi," he whispered. "You will have to wait a little more to hear it from me."

Chapter 32

It was Rabani's birthday. Her phone was beeping with birthday messages from friends and family, but the one message she had been waiting for was yet to flash on her mobile screen.

'You are going to surprise me again today, it seems. I hope you remember it's my birthday,' she looked at her mobile screen. She brought two cups of coffee from the canteen and woke Resham up, who had been sleeping in a chair next to Bunny. Resham took the cup from Rabani and hugged her saying, "Happy birthday, Rabi. May all you dreams come true."

"Thank you,*di,*" Rabani smiled. "I hope you could catch up some sleep. Bunny seems to be fine now; he slept peacefully all night."

Resham smiled with relief and said, "You should go home and take some rest before you go to work."

Rabani finished her coffee and left for home, but she could hardly sleep as she started getting calls. First, it was mom, then dad and Mannat.

Mannat was puzzled when she got a very normal reaction from Rabani. 'Is she okay with whatever is going on?' She wondered.

Barkat called her up to wish her too. A few friends and colleagues wished her as well. Rabani realized that she had to leave for Kolkata for a presentation the next day, so she started packing her bag.

'I might get too busy in the evening. Perhaps Nihal has made some plans for the evening. Besides, he too is leaving for Hong Kong, so I will get to spend some time with him,' she thought as she packed her bag. She then got ready and left for office.

Nihal got up the next morning, got ready and left for the airport. He was feeling much better after a sound sleep. He couldn't wait to see Rabani. He booked the earliest possible flight to Bangalore. 'I have already lost so much time. No more delay now. I am going to ask her today itself if she would be kind enough to marry me. Once back from Hong Kong, I will ask Papa to meet her parents. Papa likes her too. I am sure Ma is going to like her as well," he kept thinking all the time.

On reaching Bangalore, he finished all the work as quickly as possible and then realized that he's got to buy a gift and a cake for her.

Nihal knew what he wanted to buy that day. Rabani was admiring love bands at a store at the Airport one day. When she saw Nihal approaching, she had moved to another counter, but Nihal had noticed that.

'That day, I was not sure if I should buy this or not, but I will surely buy it today.' He got inside the store and picked up a pair of love bands. He tried one of them on his finger. It looked beautiful and he didn't feel like removing it.

"Congratulations, Rabi. I belong to you now. At least from my side, I am yours forever," he said and kissed the band.

He got the other one packed and kept it in his pocket carefully. "Get ready for a roller coaster ride with me, Ms. Sandhu."

By late afternoon, Nihal had reached home. 'She must be at her office,' he thought and put his phone on charging. There were many missed calls from Neil. He called Neil back, but he didn't answer the call. 'He must be busy,' Nihal thought. He dialled Rabani's number, but then disconnected immediately, 'Let me go and see her directly. I am sure she is thinking that I might have forgotten her birthday,' he thought and got into the shower.

At Rabani's office, a small birthday party was arranged for her, as was the tradition. Rabani gave a treat to her team. She showed them her nephew's pictures when a colleague asked for them. Scanning through the pictures, she came across one that Mannat had sent. It was a screenshot of a Facebook post. She took a minute to read it and a few more to understand. She couldn't believe her eyes. Her world came crashing down around her. She held on to a table close by, feeling as if there was no strength left in her body. She couldn't believe what she was seeing.

'Is this what Nihal has been wanting to tell me? Is this why he has been missing since yesterday?' she stared at her phone. 'How could he do this to me? Do I mean nothing to him?'

Rabani realized she was at her office and that too among so many people at her own birthday party. She excused herself from the party, informed her office and left for home. On the way, she got a call from Resham that Bunny was fine and would be discharged by that evening, so Rabani didn't need to go to the hospital.

As soon as she entered her house, she crashed down in the living room, as if she had no energy left in her. She was too shocked to cry, sob or scream. Memories that she had shared with him over the last two years flashed in front of her eyes.

'Two years back on this very day, Nihal had told me that he loved me and couldn't imagine his life without me. I too surrendered myself completely to his love. How am I going to live now?' She didn't realize for how long she kept sitting there. It was all dark both inside and outside her self.

The door bell rang. Resham di seemed to be back. She got up quickly, washed her face, gathered herself and opened the door. Nihal was standing at the door with a cake and flowers in his hands. That was the last thing she had expected that day.

"Happy birthday, Rabi," he shouted with joy and hugged her.

"Thanks," she moved away. She looked at his hand; a gold band was shining on the third finger of his left hand.

"Congratulations, Nihal."

"Thank you,"Nihal replied, thinking that she was referring to the landing fiasco from the day before.

"When did it happen?" Rabani asked.

"Yesterday, don't you know?" Nihal was busy setting up candles on the cake.

"The ring is beautiful," Rabani said painfully, pointing at the ring.

"Yea, thanks," Nihal looked at the ring. "See, I've got to tell you something," Nihal said after having fixed the candles on the cake.

"I already know, Nihal. I am happy…for you," she said as she tried to fight her tears. "Your parents must be very excited."

"Hmm and you?"

"I told you, I am happy for you. May god bless you both with lots of happiness in life." Rabani was on the verge of breaking down.

Nihal looked up in surprise and found her staring at his ring. He understood what she was thinking. He thought of extending the joke for some more time. "Thank you, Rabi. That's really sweet of you."

"Where is she from?"

"Delhi," he replied.

"When is the wedding, Nihal?"

"5th January," he replied, recollecting Barkat's wedding date. "You have to be there, Rabani."

'How can he be so heartless?' Rabani thought.

"My parents were insisting that I get married. Family pressure, you know. Then I too thought that it was high time I should settle down with someone. My dad knows the girl and her family, so it took no time to make the decision." Nihal tried to hide his smile.

"Yea, good," Rabani said meekly. 'How could uncle do this? He told me to be with Nihal and now he doesn't even remember that,' she thought.

"But you know, even if I marry ten times, I can't leave you, Rabi. So it doesn't matter who I am married to and who my wife is. I will always love you, Ms. Sandhu." Nihal tried to hold her close. He wanted to tell her the truth before she started crying, but that was the final blow for Rabani.

"Shut up, Nihal. What do you think I am, your mistress or a pass-time? Is this what you think about me?" Rabani shouted. "Get out of my house and my life right now. You can't insult me like this. I loved you and expected nothing in return but love and respect. But what you said just now, I am ashamed of myself; you can't be the man I loved. You just ruined everything with your words," the anger within her broke out.

"I was joking, Rabani," Nihal tried to explain. "No such thing has happened."

"Your family is announcing it to the whole world and you say there is no such thing?" Rabani opened the picture and threw her phone at Nihal.

"My family?" Nihal was stunned at what he saw. There was a post from his mother announcing his engagement.

"Be a man at least and tell the truth, Nihal, however bitter it is. I can live with that. But your lies, I can't live with them, especially after knowing what you think of me. So you better get lost from my house and my life. I would prefer dying over seeing you again."

She picked up the cake and the flowers and threw them out of the door. "I am dead for you, and no one celebrates dead peoples' birthdays."

She pushed Nihal out and locked the door after him. Nihal was shocked, he couldn't say a word. All he could do was to try to understand the post and hear Rabani crying inconsolably.

Nihal gathered his strength and tried to open the door using the password, but it seemed to be bolted from the inside.

He knocked at the door. "Rabi please, open the door. You can't do this to me. You've got to listen to me. I can explain it, Rabi. Please open the door."

She didn't respond. Nihal kept beating the door. "Open the door, Rabi, else I am going to break it open." He started pushing the door hard.

"Nihal, if you tried breaking the door, I will jump out the balcony and kill myself."

"No, you won't do any such thing. Rabi, please! Open the door, Rabi." Nihal was in tears now.

He hadn't expected the evening to take such a bizarre turn. He sat down outside the door. She was hurt and he could do nothing about it. Nihal kept sitting there for some time, then got up to leave. He caught the next flight to Delhi.

Neil wound up his day and rushed to see Rabani. He had been worried all day. Though Mannat had told him that Rabani sounded alright, he knew that all was not right. As he reached her floor in the building, he saw a cake and a bouquet lying in the corridor. He understood something had happened. He rang the door, bell but Rabani didn't open the door.

"Rabani," he called for her. He could hear her sobbing. "Rabani, open the door. It's me, Neil."

Rabani realized that it was indeed Neil at the door, not Nihal, so she unlocked the door. Neil went inside to find Rabani looking terrible. Her eyes were swollen and her face was red. She had been crying for hours, it seemed.

"Are you okay, Rabi?"

"It's all over, Neil," she said weakly. "Nihal had come here to tell me that he got engaged, flaunting his engagement ring."

'How can you be so insensitive, Nihal?' Neil thought. He dialled Nihal's number but his phone was off since he was in the flight.

Neil tried to console Rabani, but no words could comfort her that day. "I won't leave him. He can't get away with this."

"It's okay, Neil.He did what he thought is right. Besides, he had told me long back that he wouldn't be able to marry me. I want to go away from here. Nihal lives nearby and I don't want to see him again, Neil. I need to go away from here."

"Yes, Rabi." Neil was relieved that she was not crying at least. "You come with me, I will take you to Delhi tomorrow."

She nodded, "I will come with you, but I won't go to Delhi. I can't go there, Neil. Right now, I don't want to see anyone. Mannat had warned me about him and my parents, I don't want them to see me in this state. I can't go there." She was talking more to herself than to Neil. "I have a meeting in Kolkata tomorrow, so I will go to Kolkata."

"But they are your family, Rabi," Neil tried to reason with her. "Besides, you are not in the state to go anywhere alone."

"You don't worry, Neil. I am stronger than you think. I will be fine." Rabani was firm on her decision and started dumping her things in her bag.

Resham arrived home with Bunny. Rabani informed her that she would be out for a few days. She took her luggage and left with Neil.

Chapter 33

Nihal reached home late in the night. His father had not been expecting him, so he was a little surprised to see him. He didn't look okay so he asked, "Are you alright, Nihal? How come you are here today?"

Nihal sat down on a chair and held his head between his hands.

"Never mind, it's good that you are home. Will you have something? Did you have any dinner?"

Nihal shook his head. Prof. Nirmal got worried. "What has happened, Nihal? You seem upset?"

Nihal was still quiet.

At last, he spoke, "Papa, why can't things be alright with us? How long do we have to suffer for? I try to leave my past behind, but my bad luck never leaves me alone."

He started crying, hiding his face in his hands. Prof. Nirmal hugged him.

Nihal started crying even louder. "You know, papa, at times I feel that instead of Niharika, I should have been the one to die. Ma loved her more than me. Niharika is gone, still Ma loves her more still. I am here, but she doesn't care."

Prof. Nirmal tried to console him, "No, Nihal. She loves you both. Why do you think so?"

"No, she doesn't. No one loves me. Even the girl I loved more than anything in this world doesn't love me. She asked me to get out of her life. She thinks I cheated her. I love her, Papa. Ma ruined it all, Papa. Why did Ma post on Facebook that I am getting married?" Nihal was wailing like a child by this time.

Prof. Nirmal let Nihal say whatever he was holding in his heart. All he could understand was that Nihal loved someone. 'But who is she? Is he talking about Rabani or some other girl?' he wondered.

Neena heard the noise in the living room, so she came out to see what was going on too. All she saw was Nihal crying inconsolably and her husband trying to comfort him. She walked up to Nihal and hugged him.

"Why are you crying, Nihal? What is bothering you, my *bachcha*? Why do you think Ma doesn't love you? I love you, my child. I love you more than anything else in this world," Neena started crying too.

Prof. Nirmal held her. "Yes, you do Neena. You always have."

After talking his heart out, Nihal slept off when his father assured him that all would be fine. It was just matter of time, though Prof. Nirmal still didn't know who 'she' was.

On the other hand, Rabani couldn't sleep even for a minute and kept picking pieces of her broken heart and shattered dreams. 'Where did I fail? Was my love not enough for him? I never asked for anything from him, but do I deserve this?'

Neil called Mannat up and told her about Rabani's state and that Nihal had come to meet Rabani to tell her about his engagement. "I am feeling guilty, Mannat. I couldn't do anything for Rabi. I will never forgive Nihal for this. I won't see his face ever again."

"I shouldn't have sent that post to Rabi." Mannat was heartbroken too.

"It doesn't matter anymore, when Nihal himself came and told her. We couldn't have avoided it anyway," Neil consoled her. "Now we have to take care of Rabi. I don't know how she will cope with it. I am worried, Mannat. She is going to Kolkata tomorrow. I will try to get her to Delhi once she is back."

The next morning, Nihal got up and left for Bangalore, saying that he had a lot of things at hand to sort out. Rabani caught a flight to Kolkata and before leaving, asked Neil not to tell about this to anyone at home. Prof. Nirmal was trying to find out about the 'she' whom Nihal had mentioned. He called Neil up, thinking that he would know. However, when Neil saw Nihal's Delhi number flashing on his screen, he thought that the call was from Nihal, so he didn't take it. Nihal tried calling Rabani too, but she seemed to have blocked his number.

Nihal went to Rabani's house, but Resham told him that she had gone to Kolkata for a few days. He was disappointed. He asked Resham to inform Rabani that he had come for her, in case she happened to call. It was the first time in all those months that Rabani was mad at him.

He asked his office to cancel the course for him in Hong Kong, but they refused. Later, he too thought that he should perhaps give Rabani sometime. 'She can never remain mad at me for too long. I am sure she will be alright in a day or two and will call back.' Convincing himself of this, he left for Hong Kong.

Rabani immersed herself in work. She didn't want to sit idle and think about Nihal. She tried to hate him, but she couldn't. The more she tried not to think about him, the more miserable she felt. On one occasion, she thought of taking her life, but then the thought of her parents stopped her. "I have hurt my mom enough already. I can't do this to her." She called up her brother and asked whether that job opening in England that he had mentioned before was still available. 'It would be in everyone's interest if I go away from here,' she thought.

Mannat mentioned Nihal's engagement to her mother and also revealed that Rabani loved him. "I am worried for Rabani, mom. I don't know how she is taking all this? I think she should come to Delhi for a few days."

Maninder was shocked. "I never expected this. I had an idea that Rabani liked him, but I thought that Nihal liked her too. How could he do this to a girl like Rabani? My child never asks for anything." She started crying.

While in Hong Kong, Nihal tried to contact Rabani and Neil almost every day, but they didn't take his call. Rabani changed her contact number so that he wouldn't be able to reach him. He called up Barkat, but she too had no clue as she was busy at the hospital and with her wedding preparations. Calling up Mannat was a bad idea, he thought. Once, he called up at Rabani's house in Delhi, but Maninder warned him not to call again. He left a message with Resham for Rabani to call him, but Rabani never called back.

Resham sensed that something was wrong between Rabani and Nihal, so she asked Rabani one day, "Where is Nihal? We don't see him at all these days."

"Nihal is getting married,*di*. So he must be busy with the preparations at home," Rabani tried to sound normal.

"He asked me to tell you to call him," said Resham.

"Oh, I have been stormed with work for the last few days, so I couldn't talk to him. Never mind, I will meet him later," Rabani said, trying to hide her emotions.

Though Rabani tried to hide it, Resham sensed the pain in her voice. Resham had always believed that Nihal loved Rabani and the two would marry soon. She had been noticing a change in Rabani's behaviour for the last few days. Rabani was not eating properly and was coming back late from office too. Sometimes, she was up all night. She avoided meeting Neil as well and made an excuse many times whenever he came home to meet her. So, Resham too got mad at Nihal now and stopped taking his calls.

Meanwhile, Maninder kept insisting for Rabani to come to Delhi, as it had been long since she last visited home. She told whatever had happened to Tejas and Samaira too.

"Tejas, you only can do something. She is running away from everyone. I am worried for her. Every time she calls, she says she is busy at work. She doesn't come on Skype either. I know that if you will ask her to come home, she definitely will."

"No wonder she asked me to look for a job in London for her," Tejas told his mother. "Mom, I am coming to Delhi the coming Friday and I am sure to get Rabi with me."

Then he called Rabani and told her, "I am coming to Delhi next Friday, see if you can make it too. I will be there for two days. It has been long since I last saw you."

Rabani wanted to go home too, as it had been weeks since she visited her parents last. Besides, she knew that Tejas was the only one she could confide in. So, Rabani decided to go to Delhi.

Chapter 34

Nihal finished his course in Hong Kong and came back to India. When he had left, he had no idea that Rabani would be upset with him for so long. He had thought that she would forget everything in a few days and would call back, but it seemed she was really hurt and very upset. 'No matter how mad she is at me, I am sure that the moment she sees me, she will forget everything. She can't remain upset with me for too long,' Nihal assured himself while on the flight.

He landed in Bangalore and hurried to Rabani's house first thing. However, she was not at home, she had gone to Hyderabad. Instead, he met Resham who was not very happy to see him.

"Where is Rabani? How is she?" Nihal stormed Resham with questions.

"She is not here," Resham replied dryly. "And why do you want to know about her?"

"What's wrong with you, Resham *di*? Don't you know why I want to know about her?"

"Nihal,please leave her alone. She is already going through so much. Don't add to her agony by being around."

"And what about me? Do you have any idea what I am going through?"

"What about you? You go get married, but leave her alone."

"Who said that I am getting married?"

"Rabi told me that."

"She is mad. How can I marry someone else when I love her? How can I even think of that? How can she or anyone of you think that way? Do you know how much you all have hurt me?"

Resham's expressions changed. "Nihal, are you serious? I think she should know this."

"She is not ready to listen to me. She is not taking my calls. Neil is not taking my calls. You too were doing the same. How should I explain it to her?"

"Please go and tell her this, Nihal. She has nearly killed herself thinking that you have dumped her," Resham told him.

"*Di,* will you please call her from your number? I haven't heard her voice for almost a month."

Resham dialled Rabani's number and put the phone on speaker mode. Rabani answered the call. "All well,*di*?"

"Yea, Rabani. I just wanted to know when you are coming back."

"*Di,* I was about to call you about this. I am going to Delhi tomorrow. Tejas is coming from England and it has been long since I went home."

"Rabi, Nihal has come here and he wants to speak to you," Resham said.

"*Di,* it seems the network is weak. I will speak to you later," she said and disconnected the call.

Nihal's eyes grew wet. "She doesn't even want to hear about me."

"It's okay, Nihal. She knows nothing. Don't worry, I will call again and try to explain it to her."

"No,*di*. Don't tell her anything. I will go to Delhi and speak to her in person. I want to be with her, else she won't be able to handle it," Nihal told Resham and she conceded.

'Before that, I should meet Neil,' Nihal thought as he left after meeting Resham. He waited outside Neil's house. When Nihal saw Neil getting out of his car, he rushed towards him. "For how many days do you think you can avoid me?"

"Forever. You are no one to me," Neil replied sternly.

"And what about Rabani?"

"What about her? You stay away from her and from me too."

"You remember you once said that Rabi is like your sister and if I ever bring any harm to her, I will have to face you. Where is that brother today?"

"You don't deserve her, that is why I didn't come to you. Now stop following me, I am busy." Neil pushed him aside.

Instead of replying, Nihal hugged Neil. "You can't do this to me. She can't do this to me. Why are you both punishing me for something I haven't done?" Nihal was sobbing like a little child.

Neil had not expected this. He tried to push him away, but Nihal held onto him tightly, "You've got to hear me today. I am not getting married. There is no one in my life other than her."

Neil was surprised and relieved at the same time. He hugged Nihal back and got him inside his house.

"But I saw that post, Nihal. Mannat saw it on Facebook and she only sent the snapshot to me and to Rabani."

Nihal held his head in his hands. "I don't know why your wife is against me all the time. Why did she send the post to Rabani? She could have asked you or me first. Can it be possible that I am getting engaged and you have no clue about it? Besides, telling this to Rabani is like killing her," he sighed. "You know about Ma. She posted it in a misjudged excitement." and Nihal told him whatever had happened at his place that night and how his mom had made that post on Facebook and his father deleted it later, after she slept.

"But Rabi said that you told her that you got engaged. And what about the ring you have on your finger?" Neil asked, pointing at the ring.

"Oh this, this definitely is my engagement ring, my commitment to myself and to Rabi that I belong to her," Nihal told him about the plane incident and how it had made him feel when he landed safely. "That day I learnt that if she is with me, I can fight anything. I had gone to buy a ring for her, but I bought the pair instead and once I put mine on, I didn't feel like parting with it." Nihal showed him the other ring. "When I had her with me, I didn't have a ring for her. Now that I have the ring, she is not with me," he said sadly.

"It's okay. I am sure she will be with you soon," Neil tried to appease him.

"Yea, I know she can't stay away from me for too long either." Nihal wiped his face and kept the ring back in his pocket. "How is she?" Nihal asked.

"I haven't seen her since that day, Nihal. I was too embarrassed to face her. Once in a while, she calls her mom. I tried speaking to her, but she always says that she is busy and would talk later, but she never calls back. I went to see her a few times, but she was either not at home or pretended to be sleeping. Her mom, dad, Mannat and I, we are all worried for her. I hope she is fine. I told Resham to take care of her."

"Hmm, she is in Hyderabad and going to Delhi tomorrow." Nihal sighed. "I too will go to Delhi tomorrow to meet her. This time, I won't let her go anywhere."

"You know, you are mad," Neil hugged him. "I will speak to Rabani."

"You won't tell her anything. I have messed it up and only I will clean it. Let her hear it from me."

Neil patted his back. "Okay, you go speak to her and let me know if you need me anytime. I too am reaching there tomorrow. Hopefully, we will have a reason to celebrate. Just a heads up! People are all out to kill you in Delhi," Neil laughed.

"Oh! Mrs. Mannat Dhaliwal? Who cares? She is not dangerous now. She is no longer a Sandhu." Nihal replied and both started laughing.

Chapter 35

Tejas landed in Delhi and as Rabani had asked him, he waited for her at the airport itself. He had been worried for her even since he came to hear about Nihal's engagement. Samaira had told him that Rabani liked Nihal.

'I just hope she is alright,' he thought.

He had never expected Nihal to be such a creep. When Samaira had told him about Nihal and Rabani, he was happy for Rabani, but today, he was worried for his little sister who never revealed to anyone what she was going through.

Rabani reached Delhi and found Tejas waiting for her. She hugged her brother, as she was seeing him after months.

"How are you, Rabi?You look weak?" Tejas asked.

"I am fine, Veerji," she started crying as she spoke.

Tejas understood that she was lying. "Let's have coffee before we go home," he suggested and took her to a café. "Rabi, I am still that same Veerji of yours whom you used to confide in." He wanted her to talk her heart out to him before they went home.

"I don't have anything to say, Veerji. I don't know what to say." She was struggling to find words. "I tried to make some choices in life and I failed. I was always honest and sincere, and I thought he was too."Tears rolled down her eyes. "I want to go away from here, Veerji. Can I come to England with you? I want to start afresh. I have been saving money for my fellowship. I can work there for another year or so and then pursue my doctorate once I have sufficient funds."

"Stop crying, you are a brave girl. And yes, you are most welcome to come and stay with me. I have always wanted that and have told dad about it too. You don't need to work to fund your fellowship either. I can look after that."

He paused for a minute. "If you want, I can speak to Nihal and his family," Tejas said with brotherly care.

"No!" she retorted. "You won't speak to anyone for me, Veerji. Besides, I don't want to be with him anymore. I don't want you to ask anyone for anything, not for me at least, Veerji."

Tejas held her close and said, "You won't cry now. I can't see you like this. Mom would be heartbroken too if she sees you crying."

Rabani wiped her face and finished her coffee.

"Veerji, there is more to it. I hope you won't be mad at me," Rabi weighed her words. "Nihal had borrowed some money from me as he wanted to buy a house in Bangalore and he needed some funds. That house is in both of ours' name. He tried to return the money many times, but I refused because my name was there in the deed too. But now, there is no point in buying that house in a joint name. If you can speak to him for me, I want him to return my money whenever he can, there is no hurry, and I would sign the papers so that he can be the sole owner of the house. I could have sorted this out myself, but I don't want to meet him at the moment."

Tejas thought for a while. "Don't worry, you will get your money back. I will arrange to sort this out legally too. You won't need to see him for this. But don't tell anyone at home about it. I will speak to him one of these days. Now, don't think about any of this." He got up to take her home.

Maninder was relieved to see Rabani, though it did worry her to see her pale face. She hugged Rabani and complained, "Are you annoyed with me? I know you all are grown up, holding important positions in your respective offices, but you still are my kids for me and I think I have all the right to scold you. Don't I?"

Instead of Rabani, Tejas hugged his mother and replied, "You do, mom.You always do."

Mannat and Col. Sandhu joined them too.

"What is there for dinner, mom? I am starving," said Tejas. "And I am sure Rabi is hungry too."He turned to look at Rabani.

"Yes, Mom. I am famishing," Rabani tried to look cheerful.

"Two minutes, the food is ready. Meanwhile, you two freshen up," Maninder said and went to the kitchen.

Tejas and Rabani started playing with Sooraj. Sooraj grabbed Rabani's pendant which Nihal had given her. She hadn't been able to part with it, though she had tried. That day too, she gently pulled it away from Sooraj's grip.

At the dinner table, Col. Sandhu was talking about Asis, and how he used to play with him during his stay in

England, and now he had little Sooraj to play with here. Rabani was lost in her thoughts, staring at the chair in which Nihal used to sit whenever he dined with them.

"Why are you not eating? You look so pale," Maninder said, looking at Rabani's plate.

"I am eating," she said and filled her spoon.

Mannat felt upset seeing Rabani in this state. "I warned you that he is not the guy to be with. He was always a flirt, but you never listened to me."

No one had expected this.

"Yes, you warned me. But I was an idiot and didn't listen to you. See, I am paying for it. I am sitting here and simply listening to you and to everyone else," Rabani shouted. Tears rolled down her cheeks. She got up from her chair and ran to her room.

"I am warning everyone, no one will bring Nihal up in front of her. She is already going through a lot. I don't want anyone to talk about this or him anytime here," Tejas said in a firm tone and got up from his chair. "And Mannat, if you can't say anything to comfort her, please keep quiet."

Col. Sandhu signalled him to sit down. "Let me go and speak to her," he said as he picked up Rabani's plate and went to her room.

Rabani was sobbing, lying on her bed. Col. Sandhu sat next to her and stroked her head. "What is this, Rabi?"

"I am sorry, dad. I am really sorry, I failed you. I failed your upbringing. I am sorry," Rabani cried loudly and hugged her father.

"No Rabi, you have not," he hugged her back. He tried to comfort her, but her sobbing didn't stop.

"You always trusted me, gave us all the freedom to make our own choices and take our own decisions, but I failed. I can't face you, I can't face anyone. I know that you, mom, Tejas, Mannat, everyone is worried for me. Dad, I didn't do it knowingly. I had faith in my decision, but my belief has fallen flat on my face today."

Col. Sandhu held her tight. When she calmed down a bit, he said, "Rabi, when you all were growing up, I taught you to take your own decisions and learn to live with them, but I never meant to make you think that all your choices will always be right. Sometimes, you make a choice and it proves to be wrong, but then you should learn to either live with it or move on as soon as possible. This episode is one such decision in your life that didn't go the way you thought it would, but that doesn't mean that your life should stop here. All you need to do is to learn from your mistake and move on." Rabani's crying stopped and she sat down to listen to her father.

"And what is this that you can't face anyone? You have done nothing wrong. Why are you running away from everyone? *Beta*, your family is your bigger strength in these testing times. Your family never judges you on these things."

Rabani was calm now.

Col. Sandhu wiped her face. "Rabi, as far as making a wrong choice goes, it's not only you who was wrong. Your mom and I were wrong too in thinking that he was the right choice for you. We too have failed here," he sighed. "Let me tell you one more thing; it's not your loss, it's Nihal's loss.

He can never find a better girl than you and I really mean it." Col. Sandhu kept her plate in front of her and asked her to eat.

Rabani nodded and started eating her food. Col. Sandhu was relieved.

He patted her back and said, "After you finish your meal, I expect you to go and make up with your sister. I don't advocate what she said. She is simply worried for her kid sister and you know how she gets when she is upset."

Rabani nodded.

"I pity Neil. In few days, she will go back to him and you can imagine how his life is going to be," he tried to make Rabani laugh.

Rabani started smiling. "Thanks, Dad."

"Finish your dinner, we are all waiting for you outside."He got up to leave and stopped near the door, "Can I ask you for a favour?"

Rabani looked at him inquisitively.

"Can you make me a cup of coffee? I am so bored of your mom's coffee. She doesn't make it as good as you do."

Rabani nodded and got up to go out.

"She is fine now," Col. Sandhu told everyone as he joined them in the dining room. "But I want you all to behave normally with her. No more discussions about Nihal now," he looked at Mannat as he said it.

She nodded and said that she was sorry. Rabani brought coffee for everyone and sat down with her mom after handing over the coffee to everyone.

"What is Sooraj doing?" Rabani looked at Mannat.

"He is sleeping, but he will be up soon. And today, I want his *maasi* to be with him through the night. She should also know how naughty he is."

Maninder patted Rabani's back and hugged her.

Chapter 36

Late on Friday night, Nihal reached Delhi too. 'Today, I at least know that you are in Delhi. It's just that I have to reach you. I promise, you won't be mad at me any more once I am in front of you, Rabani. I never imagined that you could stay annoyed at me for this long. But besides the staying away part, I like it. I want to see how far you can go.' Nihal kept thinking about Rabani all night, though he had no idea how he would meet her alone.

He was not sure if he should go to her house, as her parents were there too. 'No worries, I will find out a way,' he convinced himself.

The next morning, he was woken up by a phone call. It was from Col. Sandhu's number. He was hopeful that he would be able to see Rabani. He took the call, but to his disappointment, it was Tejas on the other side.

"Nihal, if you are free anytime this weekend, I would like to meet you. I can come to Bangalore if you want," he said.

"No, I am in Delhi itself, Tejas. I can come to your place whenever you say."

"That's good. I will see you at Vasant Vihar's Café Coffee Day at 11," Tejas said.

Nihal was disappointed; he knew that Rabani won't be there. 'Never mind, I will explain it to her brother first,' he thought.

Tejas got ready and was all set to leave. He told Rabani that he was going to see Nihal.

"Veerji, please don't lose your temper when you meet him. I don't want you to fight with him, as I don't want any problems between us. Don't ask him for any explanation. It's his decision and we should respect it."

"Don't worry, Rabi. I won't do any such thing. Besides, I don't want mom and dad to know about this meeting."

At 11 o' clock, Nihal was sitting in front of Tejas. He had met Rabani there many times in the past. They had spent many afternoons there. "How's everyone at home, Tejas?And how are Samaira and Asis?" He asked.

"Nihal, that's not important," Tejas said. "I don't want to talk about what happened between you and Rabi, but Rabi told me that you owe her some money. Since you have now made your choice, it'll be better if you return her money. You can take some time, but do it sooner than later. In return, she is ready to sign the documents to make you the sole owner of the house. She doesn't want any complications."

Nihal was stunned. He couldn't believe his ears. She wanted to snap all ties with him, without even giving him a chance to explain. 'Rabi, you have gone too far this time,' he thought, feeling terribly hurt.

Tejas kept talking, but Nihal heard nothing. 'I will return her money as soon as possible, Tejas,' Nihal said and got up to leave.

"One minute, Nihal. It's better you stay away from all of us, especially Rabani. I don't want to see you around her ever again. She has already suffered a lot and I don't want her to be troubled anymore. It won't be good for you," Tejas warned Nihal.

Nihal couldn't listen any further and left.

Rabani had been waiting eagerly for Tejas at home. "What happened with Nihal, Veerji?" She asked when he returned.

"Nothing much, he just said that he would return the money soon. And don't worry, he won't bother you ever again."

"Thank you, Veerji."

He smiled and patted her cheek. "You should relax now too. I will mail you the details of the job openings in London soon. You can go through them and decide."

'I'll have to start all over again,' Rabani thought.

Nihal was hurt having learnt what Rabani wanted. 'She thinks I have taken her money, then what about everything else that we shared between us? How can she or I ever return them? You killed me with this, Rabani. What shall I do now?' His mind was flooded with the thoughts of the moment when Rabani had told him that she would never leave him anytime for anything. His eyes welled up. 'I can return your money, but can you return my love and affection? You will have to face me and tell me if you can return everything that was there between us.'

Nihal had told Prof. Nirmal that he would be back by afternoon. When he did not return well past evening, Prof. Nirmal got worried. He dialed his mobile, but Nihal didn't respond.

He finally called Neil. "Neil, I have been trying to contact Nihal. He has been out since morning and said that he would be back by afternoon. Do you have any idea where he could be?"

Neil had just landed in Delhi. "Uncle, I will find out and let you know."

He called Nihal up. "Where are you? And how are things?" he asked as soon as Nihal answered the call.

"I don't know, Neil," Nihal sounded miserable. "She ruined everything."

"But where are you? You dad is worried. For heaven sake, please tell me where you are."

"I don't know," Nihal shouted.

"Nihal. Listen to me carefully. Your dad is not well. Please go back home," Neil lied. He knew that only that could work on him at that time.

"What happened to Papa?" Nihal regained his senses. "I am coming home."

Neil reached Nihal's place and told his father what he had told Nihal. "Uncle, I am sorry I had to lie to him. He didn't sound very well to me on the phone. I had thought that he would sort out everything today, but something is wrong apparently. He has been struggling hard to fix up the issues in his life for the last few days."

"What issues, Neil?"

"Uncle, he loves a girl."

"Are you talking about Rabani?" Prof. Nirmal interrupted. "Though Nihal never told me about this, but I know that he has feelings for her and she too feels the same way for him." He paused. "But what issues are you talking about?"

Before Neil could talk any further, they saw Nihal entering the living room. He rushed to his father and hugged him. "What happened to you, Papa? I was so worried. Now you don't do this to me please."

"And what are *you* doing to all of us? What do you have to say about that?" Prof. Nirmal sighed and pushed him away. "For once, can we sit down and discuss what is going on here."

"Uncle, it's about…" Neil tried to explain.

"No," Prof. Nirmal gestured at him to keep quiet. "Let him speak. For how long are you going to shield him? As a father, do I have any right to know what is going on in his life? Or does he think that I don't deserve to know?"

"Sorry, Papa."

Prof. Nirmal gave him some water and asked him to sit down. He went inside and said something to his wife before coming back. "You two, come with me."

Neil and Nihal followed him out. He took them to a park.

"Can we talk, Nihal?" He asked. "It's been months now that you have been hiding whatever is going on in your life. Now I want my son to tell me what is bothering him. I have given you enough time, but today I want to hear it all."

"Papa, it's too late now. There is nothing left that I can tell you or that we can save."

"Whatever, I still want to know everything," Prof. Nirmal insisted.

So, Nihal had to tell him the truth about Rabani and himself, how he had met her, how much they loved each other, and how he was scared of getting married and how things went wrong from there.

Prof. Nirmal heard it all patiently. After getting to know everything, he said, "You are foolish, Nihal. Why is there nothing left to save? I can go and speak to Rabani's dad and explain the entire situation to him."

"No. Papa. What is the point of it if she doesn't want me anymore? Moreover, she would think that I am doing this because I don't want to return her money. Let me return her money, then I will speak to her."

"Nihal, who said she doesn't want you? See, it has already been too late. You haven't seen Rabani in a long while. She is going through hell too. Mannat told me just this morning that Rabani is not well at all and everyone at her place is worried for her. She looks doomed," Neil sighed. "You can't delay it any longer. What if something happens to her? Would you want that? If it's all about money, I will transfer the amount to her account right away."

"No, you won't do any such thing. Please give me some time. Let me arrange for the amount to return to her. A little time is all I need. Till then, no one is going to say anything to her," Nihal said firmly.

Prof. Nirmal thought for a minute and said, "I have a better solution. I will give you the money and you return it to her and clarify the things between you two."

"No, papa. I can't take your money. She once told me that it takes a lot of effort to earn money, so you shouldn't waste it. I would advise you the same."

"Nihal, I agree with her, but what good will be this money if something happens to you or to her. You have already suffered a lot and she has suffered so much as well. What if something happens to her? You should thank your lucky stars that she didn't do anything stupid. You know, she was all alone there in Bangalore." Prof, Nirmal explained, "You can take the money as a loan from me and return the amount back whenever you have sufficient funds."

Nihal thought about it for a minute, then agreed.

"If all is good, then let's go and speak to Rabani," Neil got up hurriedly.

"No, Neil, Not now. Let me transfer the money to her account and speak to her first. Let her decide if she wants to come back at all first. I don't want to force her. She has walked away from me. I want her to come back on her own."

"I agree with him, Neil. But don't take too long, Nihal," said Prof. Nirmal as he got up. "Let's go home. Because of you two, I am away from my wife and I can't keep her waiting. Your company is not good for my married life."

They started laughing.

Back home, Neena was waiting for them. "Where were you all? You took so long, I was worried."

"Your sons tried to spoil me by taking me out for a boys' night out, but I was missing my pretty wife so much that I came back," he cheered Neena up.

"When will you stop flirting, Professor?" Neena smiled.

Nihal missed Rabani. She too used to say so, he thought.

Chapter 37

After dinner that night, Nihal was sitting with his father. Neena was sleeping after having had her medicine.

"I am happy for you, Nihal. Finally, you found what I wanted you to have in life; someone to love you and stand by you, like I have Neena with me."

"You love Ma a lot, Papa. However badly she behaves, I have never seen you getting mad at her."

"Because you don't know what she has done for me," he replied. "At one time, she left everything for me, even when I had nothing to give her."

"Really, Papa?"

"Your Ma and your *maasi*, Neera, were your Preet *bua*'s friends. I am sure you know that."

Nihal nodded.

"I had been seeing Neena right from the time when we were kids. She and your *maasi* used to come home with Preet. We all grew up together and whenever they stayed at our place till late, I used to walk them home. Your *Nanaji* was a businessman and had a famous sweet shop in Amritsar. We were not very good financially in comparison. I didn't realize when I developed a liking for her, and she for me. But neither of us told the other about it. She used to pull my leg all the time over something or the other-that I was a bookworm, I never smiled, or that I was scared of girls." Prof. Nirmal smiled as if he was living those days again.

"Then?" Nihal was curious.

"I was doing my M.Sc. and Neena was in her second year of graduation. One day, Preet told me that Neena's parents were planning to get her married. I was shattered but kept quiet, because I knew the difference between our families' social status. Then one day, Preet said that Neena didn't want to get married as she liked someone else. My heart skipped a beat. 'She likes you, Veerji,' she said. I didn't know what to say, so I just avoided talking about it and sternly told Preet not to bring up anything about her again."

"Then how did you two get married?"

Prof. Nirmal smiled and continued, "One day, your Ma asked me if I would marry her, as her father would not wait for too long. I didn't know what to say, so I just shook my head in a no. Then I came to know that she had refused to marry the boy that her father had chosen for her, and for that she had even got a beating at home."

"Ohh." Nihal felt bad.

"I gathered my courage and went to meet your Nanaji. I requested him to listen to her and to not hit her at least. I requested him to wait for a year or two, after which the two of us could marry."

Nihal shrugged his shoulders, "Then?"

"Your Nanaji insulted me that I should have considered the difference in our social and financial status, and that his daughters' weekly expenses were equal to my father's monthly salary. I had nothing to say, but your Ma stood by me and asked her father to not insult me. She was hit again right there in front of me, but I couldn't take that. I stood between Neena and her father. I told him that I would take her with me if he hit her again. Your Nanaji asked Neena if she wanted to go with me, and if she did, he would never see her face again. Your Ma looked at me. I told her that I couldn't give her anything of the kind of life that she had at her father's place, and she said she didn't fancy any of that and came with me."

"And the marriage?"

"She left her house with me, but then I didn't know where to take her, so I took her home. My mother was stunned to see her and knowing about her. She was worried of how my father would react. She was right. When my father came home, he got really mad at me. But then, your Tayaji explained to him that since Neena had left her house and her parents were not going to accept her back, she had nowhere else to go. In such a time, they couldn't abandon us both, so it was good and in everyone's interest that the two of us should be wedded, otherwise in what capacity could she stay with us. So, we were wedded the very next day at a *gurudwara* close to our house." Prof. Nirmal removed his glasses and wiped them.

"That's quite a thing, papa. I didn't know you were so courageous."

"That's not all, Nihal.The real deal started after this," Prof. Nirmal said, while cleaning his glasses. "We were married, but I actually had nothing to give her. I was still dependent on my father, having no income of my own. For many months thus, I couldn't buy her anything. She used to wear Preet's clothes. Then, she started taking tuition classes at home after her college hours. I too started taking tuitions, so that we could contribute something towards the house expenses. She never demanded anything. Whenever I used to feel low watching her in this state, she would always cheer me up, saying that she was happy to be with me and that if she wanted money, there was plenty at her father's place, or at that boy's house whom her father wanted her to marry. She said she liked me and that she had no regrets after seeing how much I loved her and my family cared for her. That's why I love her, Nihal." Prof. Nirmal wiped his face and wore his glasses back.

"When did you come to Delhi then, Papa? And what about Nanaji and his family?"

"Well, your Nanaji snapped all ties with your Ma and never met her again. I tried to convince her in the later years that she should go back and meet him, but she didn't budge. Your Neera maasi got married to the boy whom your Nanaji had selected for your Ma.

"You mean Raghav uncle?" Nihal was surprised. "But he has always been so nice to us."

"Yes, Raghav has been very sensible since the beginning. He never held any grudges against us. So fortunately, your Neera maasi and your Meena maasi were always in touch with her. They tried to help us many times, but your Ma politely refused each time. After I finished my M. Sc., I got a job at a college in Amritsar. By then, Neena had finished her graduation too. I got a lot of tuition work in addition, so we were a little better off by then. I remember, I bought her a saree with my first salary. You will still find it in her cupboard today. She never parted with it."

Nihal started thinking about the pendant that he had given Rabani on her birthday. 'I don't know if she still has that pendent on her or not.'

The chain of his thoughts was broken as Prof. Nirmal spoke again, "Then, your Tayaji told me about a job in Delhi, but I was hesitant. However, your Ma asked me to take up the job. She convinced me that we could do this and that she was with me. We came here and I did my Ph.D. We used to stay in a one room house, while at your Nanaji's house, she had a room all to herself. But she never complained. Then you two came into our life. She got busy with you, but she never neglected me. I am proud of her for the way she brought you two up. I wish you were as strong willed as her and not like me," Prof. Nirmal laughed.

"Why do you think so, Papa?"

"Look at you, how you messed up your life and Rabani's too. If your Ma hadn't asked me that time, I would never have dared to ask her to marry me either. That's why I said that if you were more like your Ma, you wouldn't be sitting here and thinking about Rabani," Prof. Nirmal pulled his leg. "On a more serious note, this is the reason I love your Ma so much. However difficult the times were, she never left me alone for a minute. Now when she needs me, how can I abandon her? These are the testing times in life. Do you think things will never change? I don't think so. Rabani doesn't think so."

Nihal was surprised. "What does she not think, Papa?"

"You know, when she had come home, she told me, 'Uncle, nothing will change if you won't try.' So, I started taking your Ma out of the house. She refused initially, but eventually agreed and started coming out with me to the park, the market and the yoga classes. We started seeing a new doctor and his treatment really worked for her. You can see for yourself that she is a lot better now. I am hopeful now that your Ma will be alright soon." He patted Nihal's back. "Such a bright girl, but what a pity. She is stuck with an idiot." Prof. Nirmal laughed.

"Papa," Nihal retorted. "I am not as stupid as you think. Who found that bright girl, by the way? I have just one complaint against her, that she didn't trust me. She should have asked me at least once."

"You are wrong, Nihal. Try to understand. She saw that post and then that ring on your finger. When you told her that you were forced by your parents, she didn't know that it was a prank." He paused. "Can you imagine what she has gone through? And you say that she didn't trust you."

"You are right, Papa. I am an idiot. She never got mad at me for whatever I did, but this time I think I really hurt her. At times, I wonder if I really deserve her."

"No, you surely deserve her, Nihal, because you love her the way I love Neena. Don't weigh yourself down with it. Look at the brighter side. If you hadn't played that prank, God knows how long it would have taken for all this to happen. Now, I guess it's a matter of just a few days and you will have her with you forever."

Nihal smiled at his father, "Thanks Papa, for everything."

"Anytime, son," Prof. Nirmal smiled back.

Chapter 38

Later that evening, Neil reached Col. Sandhu's house. Everything seemed fine on the surface, but he sensed that everyone was worried for Rabani.

Seeing Col. Sandhu upset, he said, "Uncle, I am sure things will work out for Rabani soon. It's just a matter of time. You don't worry. I am in Bangalore and I will take care of her."

"Why are you avoiding me, Rabi?" He asked when he met Rabani. "Do you feel that I too am a part of it?"

"No, Neil. Not even once did I think that. Nihal came to my life much later, but you are the one I have grown up with. I never doubted your intentions. You know I trust you more than Mannat."

"I know."

"Neil, you and Nihal are like brothers. I don't want you two to fall apart just because of me," she said and looked away to hide the growing wetness in her eyes. "I will try to make Mannat understand this too before she joins you in Bangalore. Give me some time, I will explain it to her."

"That won't be required, Rabi, but I appreciate your gesture. Promise me that you will not disappear ever again and will always answer my calls. Otherwise, I will feel that you blame me for it and have not forgiven me." He wiped the tear that rolled down her cheek.

Tejas returned to England after spending the day with his parents. "Mom I don't have much leave. Besides, we all are coming back for Barkat's wedding in few days anyway," he told his mother when she insisted for him to stay for few more days. Neil returned to Bangalore too after meeting Mannat and their son.

Rabani was a bit relaxed after Tejas informed her that Nihal would't bother her ever again. She could go to Bangalore without any fear, though she had decided to shift out of her existing address in Bangalore. Maninder asked her to stay with them for few more days, but she refused, saying that there was a lot of work going on at her office, assuring none the less that she would come back soon. "I have asked my office to send me to Delhi," she told her mother.

'It will be so difficult to live without him,' she thought as she boarded the plane for Bangalore alone. 'We used to fly back together each time,' her eyes welled up.

On Monday morning, Nihal transferred the money to Rabani's account. He called up Tejas to inform him about the same, but the call was received by Samaira as Tejas was sleeping.

"Please inform Tejas that I have transferred the money to Rabani's account."

"Okay, I will tell him," she replied. There was a silence for a few seconds. "Anything else you want me to tell anyone."

"Yea, tell your husband that no matter what he says, I won't stay away from Rabi. I love her and I will go and see her. If he has a problem, I don't care."

"You are engaged and going to get married soon, Nihal. It is in everyone's interest for you to stay away from her. You will ruin her life and yours as well. You know, when I heard about it, I couldn't believe it. But the fact is that you have made your choice and will now have to learn to live with it, and leave Rabi alone."

"What choice, Samaira? What choice are you talking about? She is being silly and you all have become a part of this stupid story. I am not engaged to anyone. It's just a ring that I have on my finger which has become so important that my words hold no value for anyone anymore."

"What does this mean? Are you not getting married?" Samaira was surprised.

"I will sometime, only if Rabi comes back to me. After all, I need a girl to get married to," Nihal explained.

"I still don't get it, Nihal," Samaira was confused.

"Samaira, I have loved only one girl in my life and that is Rabi,then how can I marry someone else? All of you have misunderstood me. I am not engaged to any other girl. She is the only one in my life."

Samaira was relieved. "Nihal, you should go and speak to Rabi. Whatever Tejas told me suggests that she is not fine at all. Meanwhile, I too will talk to dad and Tejas."

"Thanks for hearing me out, Samaira. I am going to see her soon. I was only waiting to sort out this money issue between us," Nihal said and hung up.

"Run away from me, Ms. Sandhu, if you can. I am on my way," Nihal whispered.

Rabani saw the message about the money being credited to her account. She knew where it had come from. She called up Tejas to inform him about it, but it was Samaira again who took the call and said, "Rabani, Nihal had called up to say that he has transferred the money."

"Did he say anything about the papers?"

Samaira had no idea about the money or the papers, still she said, "Yea, Tejas said that if Nihal comes with the papers, you meet him and sort out the issue. He said he was sure that you could do this."

"Okay," Rabani said and hung up. "I will have to face him."

Rabani contemplated on how she was going to face him and what she would say. She decided that she would stick to business and won't talk of anything other than that. She only had to see him just one last time, she thought.

Later that afternoon, Rabani received a call from an unknown number. "Hi, it's me...Nihal."

Rabani's heart skipped a beat. She was hearing his voice after months. "Hello," she replied meekly.

"I hope you checked your account statement, Rabi. I have transferred your money to your account," Nihal said, stressing on 'your money'.

"Yes, I saw the message."

"If you are free in the evening, can we meet? I want to finish this as soon as possible," Nihal said.

Rabani was heartbroken. 'He can finish it, but will I ever be able to get over it?'

"Yea sure," she replied. 'I have to do this, I have to be strong,' she told herself. "I will see you at the coffee shop near our building around six."

"Okay, see you then," Nihal replied.

When Rabani reached, she found Nihal already sitting there. 'He is always before time,' she thought.

When Nihal saw her coming, he got up to hug her, but she avoided it and sat down quickly in the chair across from his.

'She looks so pale and frail. What has she done to herself?' he thought.

Though Rabani had tried to cover up her swollen eyes and gloomy face, but her make up didn't seem to help much. She was still wearing that pendant around her neck, Nihal observed carefully. 'You love me, Rabi, and you can't deny it.'

She noticed too that the ring was still there on his finger. "Where are the papers? Lets finish this quickly, I've got to rush," she said hurriedly. She didn't want to sit there for too long. It was difficult for her to sit there, yet to not look at him.

"How are you, Rabi?"

"Good," she said. "Can I see the papers now please?"

Nihal gave her a file. She opened the file and started going through it. "These are your house papers. I am talking about the affidavit that states that I have no claim on the house."

Nihal looked at her for a moment and said, "Our house papers, Rabi. I am buying this house for you and this will always belong to you, whether you live there or not. If you are gone, what will I do with the house?"

"This is your money and this is your house. Soon, you will be married. You both could live there," she said, looking at the ring.

She didn't want to make eye contact with him, as she knew she would't be able to hide her emotions.

"Rabi, I love you and only you. I can't marry…"

She got up from her chair, "I don't need to know anything, Nihal. Whenever the papers are ready, courier them to me. I will sign and send them back."

She was about to leave, but he held her hand. "Don't go, Rabi. Listen to me at least. I love you and only you, and you love me too. Why don't you understand?"

Rabani pulled her hand away from his grasp. "I don't have anything left to do with you. Don't make a scene here. People are looking at us."

"I don't care," Nihal snapped.

"But I do care, Nihal." Rabani started walking towards the door.

"Rabi," he screamed and followed her.

Everyone in the coffee shop turned to look at them.

He caught hold of her hand again, "Why are you doing this to me? I haven't done anything. Please listen to me. I am not marrying anyone."

"Let me go, Nihal."

"Okay, if you want to go, return this to me."With his other hand he grabbed the pendant that he had given her. "I have returned your money, now you return this to me."

"No, Nihal." Rabani held the pendant tightly with her own hand. "You can't do this to me. I can't give you this." She started crying. "I will die without this."

"Stop fooling yourself, you still love me, Rabi."Nihal let go of the pendent but not her hand. "Listen to me," he shouted, "All I want you to know is that I love you and will always wait for you, whether you come back to me or not. Go wherever you want to go, do whatever you want to do. I will neither follow you, nor try to meet you. The day you realize your mistake, you will regret it, Rabi. No one can love you as much as I do," he said and released her hand.

Rabani rushed out of the shop, but Nihal kept standing there and staring at the door through which she had gone out.

Chapter 39

Rabani reached home. She was not sure about what she had heard. "He is not getting married, then why does he have that ring on his finger? He seemed to be speaking straight from his heart, but I don't understand what he means."

Rabani was trying hard to understand it all, but she could not make any sense of it. "What if what he said is right? I didn't even try to listen to him."

Resham got tea for her, but she didn't have it.

Rabani got up from her bed and went straight to Nihal's flat. She rang the doorbell a few times, but no one answered. She entered the code, unlocked the door and went inside. All his things were lying the way they used to, but he was not there. She switched on his laptop. The wallpaper was one of her and Nihal's pictures clicked during Mannat's wedding. She went through his pictures to find some from his engagement, but she didn't find any. There were mostly her pictures, and some of his family.

"Where are you, Nihal?" she tried calling him up, but his phone was switched off.

Rabani called Neil up and told him all about what Nihal had said and whatever had happened at the coffee shop.

"He was right, Rabani.There is no wedding happening for him. That post was made by his mother, and you know her state already. His father removed the post later."

"But that ring on his finger?"

"He is an idiot, you know. That ring, he said, is his commitment to you and to himself that he belongs to you. That is why he didn't remove it even after so much of trouble. We all believed in the ring and the post, but none of us believed in him," he paused. "Rabi, if he was indeed cheating on you, he could have removed the ring before meeting you, but he did not. He loves you and has suffered just as much as you did all these days. It'll be good if you sort out your differences before it's too late."

Tears rolled down from Rabani's eyes on to her cheeks.

"Rabi, you don't know this, we had nearly lost him, but he said that it was your love that brought him back," and he told her all about the plane incident. "Just be with him and hold him. He needs you and you need him too."

Rabani was shocked at this sudden turn of events. She tried to call Nihal desperately, but his phone was still switched off. Rabani was in tears. She threw her phone away, opened his cupboard and started taking out his things. She threw them on the bed and lied down over them, clinging to his clothes. She was regretting the way she had behaved. 'Nihal loves me so much, but I hurt him. I embarrassed him in front of everyone.' She hugged his pillow, trying to find him in everything around her. She called out to him loudly, "Nihal, please come back to me. I love you. Please don't go away." She felt cold, so she put on his shirt. She felt as if Nihal was holding her in his arms and she dozed off.

Resham got anxious when Rabani did not return after a long while. Her purse, shoes, jacket, even her tea, everything was lying there, but she was nowhere around. Worried, she called up Rabani's number. After many calls, she replied that she was at Nihal's place.

She was wailing loudly, "Resham *di,* I hurt him, he is gone. I am not able to find him. He said he would never come back. I want him. I love him. I am sorry, Nihal. I ruined everything."She was talking in broken sentences.

Resham got scared.

"Please find him, *di*. Please find him for me."

Resham rushed to Nihal's apartment. The door was open and Rabani was lying on his bed. She was running a high fever and was mumbling something. Resham got worried seeing her in that state. She tried calling Nihal, but his phone was off. He was actually on his way to Delhi.

It was late in the night when Resham rushed Rabani to the hospital. She had fever and was semiconscious.

Back in Delhi, Prof. Nirmal was excited to see Nihal. "How did it go? Where is Rabani? I didn't expect you to come back so soon. I thought you two would be celebrating."

"No,Papa. She is not ready to listen to me. Neil was right, Papa. She has suffered a lot. She looked so weak and miserable. I repent playing that prank on her."

"Don't worry, Nihal. Give her some time. She will listen to you, I am sure of that. And don't stop trying. Speak to her again."

"I will, Papa. I will go back the day after and try to talk to her again. Tomorrow is mom's appointment with the doctor, so I thought I would go with you this time."

"Good, have some food now and relax. I am sure she will be in a better state of mind by the day after," Prof. Nirmal assured him.

Nihal checked his phone and found a lot of missed calls. Most of them were from Rabani, but the last two were from Resham. He called Rabani back first. Her phone went on ringing, but she didn't take the call. Then, he called Resham.

"Nihal, Rabi is not well. She has a high fever and is unconscious. I got her to the hospital.If you are around, please come fast."

"Di, I am in Delhi, but I am leaving right away. Till then, please take care of her."

"Oh! If you are in Delhi, please inform Sandhu uncle too. I don't want to bother them in the night."

Nihal informed his father about it and rushed to Rabani's house. "Keep me informed," Prof. Nirmal said.

Col. Sandhu answered the door and was surprised to see Nihal there. "Uncle, Rabi is unwell and she is at the hospital. I have come to inform you. I got a call from Resham *di*. If any of you wants to come with me, I am leaving right away."

By then, Maninder too had come to the door and heard their conversation. "Thank you, Nihal, for having us informed. But you need not worry, we will see to it. You can go home," she said bitterly. She was upset.

"Auntie,what is important right now is Rabi. We can sort out our issues later, but right now I would request you to come with me. She needs you there and no one can have you reach there faster than me."

Maninder tried to speak, but Col. Sandhu stopped her. "She will come with you, Nihal. Please wait for a minute. Let her get her things."He then asked Maninder to pack her bag.

Mannat heard the noise in the living room too and came out to see what was up. The moment she saw Nihal, she was baffled. "What the hell are you doing here?"

"It is you who has ruined everything, Mannat. If you had a problem with me, you should have told me. Why did you pull Rabani into this? Do you have any idea what you have done?" He paused and shook his head. "How insensitive of you, Mannat. She is in the hospital now, courtesy you and me. God forbid if anything happens to her, I won't leave you, Mannat." Nihal had raised his voice at Mannat for the first time ever.

Mannat was stunned. She had never seen Nihal losing his cool before. Col. Sandhu intervened and asked Mannat to go inside. Maninder came back with her bag.

"I am sorry, uncle. I was just…"

Col. Sandhu patted his shoulder when Nihal tried to apologize.

"You take care of Rabi and Nihal too. I shall be here with Mannat and Sooraj," Col. Sandhu told Maninder. "Neil will be there to help you."

Maninder did as she was told and in no time, they were in a flight to Bangalore.

Chapter 40

When Nihal and Maninder reached the hospital, Rabani was lying in the hospital bed. Neil and Resham were there with her. Rabani had a high fever and was in a semiconscious state. As per the doctor, she had not been eating properly all those days and had grown very weak. They were to carry out some more tests the next morning, Neil informed them.

"I reached just an hour ago too, since I was flying. She had called me in the evening and told me that she was looking for you," Neil told Nihal.

"I met her just this evening. Had I known this, I wouldn't have left her alone. I should have stayed," Nihal murmured.

"She will be fine soon. Stay with her, she was calling out your name in her sleep."

Nihal nodded, "Anyway, you go home, Neil. You must be tired. I am here."

"Nihal, she was in a bad state when I found her. She was saying that you were upset with her. I don't know what happened yesterday. All I can say is that she loves you and she is too precious to let go for your ego or anger," Resham told Nihal when he was walking her to her cab.

"She is too precious to let go for anything,*di*. Do you think I can ever be mad at her? You don't worry, she will be fine."

When he returned back to Rabani's room, he found Maninder sitting next to her and sobbing quietly, "My child, you don't deserve any of this. Why did I listen to you and let you come to Bangalore yesterday? I should have stopped you."

Nihal consoled her, "Auntie, she is sleeping. You too should catch up on some sleep. I am here with her. I will wake you up, if needed. It won't do her any good to see you in this state."He made her sit down on the other cot in the room and sat down next to Rabani.

Rabani was holding the pendant, which Nihal had given her, with one hand and was mumbling in her sleep. She was calling out for Nihal and was pleading with him to not go away. He touched her forehead; it was burning.

"What have you done to yourself, and all because I have been an idiot?" He kissed her forehead and held her hand gently. "I am here, Rabi. How can I leave you? I can't ever, Rabi."

He kept sitting by her side, holding her hand and she kept sleeping, holding his. Soon, Rabani was peacefully asleep. Nihal dozed off in the chair next to her too, still holding her hand. Maninder was mad at him but didn't say anything as Rabani finally seemed to be at ease with him.

"Nihal, go home and relax for some time. You have been up all night. I am here with her. The doctors are here too, we will manage. Neil should be here soon as well. You have already done so much for us. Besides, you must have to go to work too," Maninder told Nihal, the next morning.

"Auntie, I am not going anywhere till Rabi is alright. I told you, we can sort out our issues later. Right now, I am not up for any discussion on this." Nihal handed her a cup of tea and sat down next to Rabani.

While clearing up the drawers, he found his shirt there. "These are the patient's clothes. You can't take them home. We will need them at the time of discharge," the nurse told him.

He was elated to find out that Rabani had been wearing his shirt. He shook his head and whispered, "So you are not mad at me, Ms. Sandhu. And I love your way of expressing it."

By that evening, Rabani's fever came down a bit and she opened her eyes. Nihal was sitting by her side and her mom was there too. She looked at Nihal and was thrilled to see him around, but she was too weak to speak and closed her eyes instead.

"Are you alright?" Nihal asked Rabani. He then informed Maninder, "She has opened her eyes, auntie. I am going to call the doctor. You be with her till then." He rushed out to summon the doctor, not noticing that Rabani was trying to hold his hand.

The Doctor came in and examined her. "She would be alright soon."

Nihal had been with Rabani all this time and hadn't left her for even a minute, unless it was something urgent. Both Neil and Resham asked him to go and take some rest, but he didn't give up. "Let her be alright first," he said.

Maninder too mellowed down a bit on seeing Nihal in this state. Besides, Neil had also told her to believe what she was seeing, and not what she had heard. "Auntie, I have known Nihal since childhood. Look at him, do you think he is cheating us?"

Whenever Rabani awoke, Nihal would get up and go to sit in the chair at the farther end of the room, and when she was asleep, he would come back and sit next to her cot again. Each time that Rabani woke up, she found him either sleeping in the chair next to her bed, or simply sitting and reading some book, or trying to cheer her mother up. He didn't try to speak to her much, except for asking her how she was or if she needed anything.

"He is mad at me and he should be. I have done no good to him," Rabani thought.

On the third day, Rabani's condition improved and she was put on oral diet. Nihal had gone to buy her medicines. Maninder was sitting with Rabani. "You look better today. You scared us all that day, Rabi."

"I am sorry, mom. I don't know how it happened."

"All thanks to Nihal who got me here. I don't think I will ever be able to understand this boy. I was so upset with him, but he didn't mind whatever I said even a bit and has looked after you as well as me all these days." She held Rabani's hand. "Rabi, I don't know what it means but when I asked Neil about Nihal's engagement, he said that there is no such thing." She waited for a while and then said ponderously, "Nihal loves you, Rabi, and I have always seen it in his eyes."

They were interrupted as Nihal was back, so she changed the topic. "Rabi seems fine today. As you told me, you should now go home Nihal, and take some rest. You have been here for the past three days."

Before Nihal could say anything, Rabani spoke, "Yes, I am okay now. You go home and take some rest. Have a peaceful sleep tonight."

"Do you really know what would bring me peace?" Nihal frowned. "I am fine, auntie. Once we are done from here, I will go back to Delhi," Nihal answered without looking at Rabani.

"Please Nihal, go for some time. I don't want you to fall sick too. We have seen enough of hospitals these days," Maninder said with authority. "At least take a shower and wear some fresh clothes. You are stinking."She swirled her nose to make him laugh.

"Okay, I will go for an hour. But first, you two have your breakfast. And I am going home because you said so, not she." He opened the box that Resham had got and kept the soup bowl in front of Rabani and asked her to finish it. Rabani followed as she was told.

Nihal went back to his place. As he entered, his room seemed to be upside down. All his clothes were on his bed. The bed sheet was crumpled. His laptop was open. He kept looking at the things for a while, then started keeping his things back in the cupboard. There, he found Rabani's phone and the scarf that she had been wearing the day he met her at the café. 'Did she come here?' he thought. He lied down on the bed holding that scarf.' Did she come looking for me? Maybe that's how she was wearing my shirt that day.' He got up, took a shower, wore fresh clothes and rushed back to the hospital. He kept the scarf in his pocket, thinking, 'You came back for me, Rabi.'

When Rabani woke up that afternoon, she saw Nihal sleeping on the cot where her mother used to sit. He seemed to be feeling cold, sleeping with holding his legs close to his chest. Rabani kept looking at him for some time. He had the same child-like smile on his face in his sleep that she loved so much. She got up from her cot and covered him with a blanket. Nihal stretched his legs inside. Rabani sat down next to him. She was looking at the man who meant everything to her. Her eyes welled up again. She fondled his hair. "I am sorry, Nihal," she whispered.

Nihal shifted in his bed. Rabani immediately got up and turned back towards her cot.

She was about to move away when Nihal held her forearm. "Rabi, don't go," he said with his eyes still closed. "I can't see you going away. You remember, you once said that you will never leave me, come what may?"He sat up on the cot and pulled her back towards him.

Rabani rested her head on his shoulder and started snivelling. "I am sorry. I have been unfair to you. I have hurt you. I was rude, unreasonable and stroppy. I should have listened to you. Please don't be mad at me. I can't stay away from you. I am sorry, Nihal," she sobbed into his shoulder while holding him tightly.

Nihal's eyes welled up too. "I can never be mad at you, Rabi. You know that. You were hurt, pained and tormented. Believe me, I have never even thought of another girl ever, not for a minute. I was just pulling your leg that day, not realizing how much it hurt you. I am sorry, Rabi. Don't ever think of leaving me. I was miserable without you." He held her face in his hands and said, "I can never go away from you. You only went away too far. All I wanted was for you to take a step towards me, and I'd cover the distance between us in no time. I love you, Rabi. I always have." He hugged her again.

All their pain, anguish and suffering washed away with their tears. Nihal got up from his cot, lifted Rabani up in his arms and placed her gently on her cot. "You need to rest, Rabi. Don't think too much. I am always there with you."He kissed over her eyelids and wiped her tears. "I want my smiling Rabi back. You have no right to make her suffer."

He took out a chain from his pocket; it had a ring as a pendant. He tied it around Rabani's neck. Pointing to the ring he said, "This is the other ring from the pair of bands which I bought for us, and it's for you." He stretched his hand, showing her the ring he was wearing. "Will you be mine forever? I got this for your birthday, but couldn't give it to you. The day you are ready, put it on your finger. I will wait for that day, Rabi."

"You will have to speak to my dad," Rabani blushed.

"That I will at the earliest," Nihal held her close. "I just have one regret," he paused, "I will miss Kritika all my life."He then started laughing.

"You are impossible," Rabani punched him hard and tried to push him away, but he hugged her.

"So, the love birds have finally made up," Neil said, standing in the doorway.

Chapter 41

Nihal called up his father and told him about Rabani, "Papa, she is fine now. If you want, you may speak to her dad now."

"And what if I don't want to?" Prof. Nirmal pulled his leg. "Tell me, what do you want?"

"Papa, please speak to Sandhu uncle."

"That's like my son. I will do it sooner than later."

Prof. Nirmal called up Col. Sandhu and told him that he wanted to see him. Col. Sandhu invited Prof Nirmal to his place, saying, "It would be a pleasure to see you."

As decided, Prof. Nirmal met Col. Sandhu that evening and explained the entire situation to him and told him why it had taken him so long to approach Rabani's family.

"We always liked Nihal for our daughter," Col. Sandhu told him.

So, it was decided that once Rabani would be out of the hospital, they would formally announce Rabani and Nihal's engagement. Col. Sandhu also informed about this meeting to his wife and son.

Back home, Prof. Nirmal asked Neena if she would like to go out on a date with him. She agreed at once.

"But Neena, promise me that you will not be scared."

"No, I won't be. I promise," she said.

The next day, Prof. Nirmal and his wife were on a plane. The plane landed and they took a cab from the airport.

"But you haven't told me where we are going," Neena said.

"Trust me, you will like it, Neena."

The cab stopped in front of a hospital. Neena got down and looked at Prof. Nirmal. Fear could be seen clearly in her eyes. He held her hand tightly and entered the hospital. Neena looked all around curiously. At the reception, he enquired about someone and took Neena to a room.

Rabani was sitting on her cot inside. She was being discharged from the hospital that day. She had just finished her breakfast and Nihal was giving her medicine. "Take your medicine and rest for a while. Meanwhile, I will complete the discharge formalities."

Maninder was sitting in the chair and looking at them lovingly, when Prof. Nirmal entered the room along with Neena. Nihal saw them and got surprised. Not only him, but Rabani too was stunned.

Gesturing at Rabani, Prof. Nirmal said, "Neena, do you know who she is?"

Neena shook her head.

"This is Rabani. She is the girl who loves your son and your son loves her too."

"You lost one *bitiya* at the hospital one day, and today we are taking home another one," Prof. Nirmal explained to her.

Neena walked up to Rabani and hugged her. "She is not Niharika. Her name is Rabani and she is not my *bitiya*. A daughter gets married and goes away with her husband, but a daughter-in-law always stays with you."

She looked at Rabani and said, "Rabani, will you come to our house with Nihal?"

Rabani turned to look at her mother, who was looking at all this in an astonished manner.

Nihal went to Maninder and said, "They are my parents, auntie. You met my dad at Mannat's wedding and she is my mom. You wanted to meet them."

Prof. Nirmal turned to Maninder. "I met your husband yesterday and asked him for your daughter's hand for Nihal, and we would be really happy if you agreed to it too. I know my son troubled you all a lot, especially Rabani, but I know one thing, Rabani will never regret her decision of being with him," he said and he patted Nihal's back.

Maninder bobbed her head in agreement.

Rabani got up from the cot, took off the chain from around her neck and gave it to Nihal, extending her hand towards him. Nihal slipped the ring on to her finger and whispered, "Now you can never run away from me, Ms. Sandhu. I have locked you forever."

Epilogue

As Nihal had said, on 5th January, along with Barkat and Sartaj, Nihal too got married to Rabani. It was of course a happy landing, but a new journey began at the same time. If you think there were no turbulences in their life there on, you'd be wrong. Life is a flight full of turbulences but together, Nihal and Rabani sailed through all the hard times. These turbulences not only made their journey interesting, but also brought them closer to each other.

About the Author

Shalu Thakur Dhillon was born in Patiala, India. She holds Post Graduation degrees in Mathematics and Education. Before taking up writing as a serious business, she was into teaching for many years.

Being wedded to an olive green got her the opportunity to live in various parts of India. Currently, she lives in Goa with her husband and two sons.

She loves reading, music, travelling and yoga. To know more about her visit her Facebook page https://m.facebook.com/thestoryteller918/. You can mail to her at thestoryteller918@gmail.com

A note to my reader

Dear reader,

That was all from my side for now. A sincere thanks to you for having the time and patience to read this book. It means a lot to me. This is my first book, the beginning of my journey as a writer. I would love to know your views and opinions about this book. Please pen down your views on the website that you have bought the book from, and feel free to write down on my Facebook page.

https://m.facebook.com/thestoryteller918/.

Your suggestions and ideas will help me improve my writing.

Signing off for now,

Shalu Thakur Dhillon